Geoff Tristram has been a cartoonist for over thirty years, w of clients including Embassy W Tarmac, Past Times, Winsor & Newton, Trivial Pursuit and the television show, 'They Think It's All Over!', to name but a few.

He has drawn or painted celebrities such as Jonathan Ross, Sir Ian Botham, Jeremy Clarkson, David Vine, Alan Shearer, Ian Hislop and Gary Lineker, not to mention virtually every famous snooker player that ever lifted a cue. You may have even noticed him at the 2006 World Championships on TV, interviewing them as he drew their caricatures.

Geoff has also designed many book covers, album sleeves for bands such as UB40, The Maisonettes and City Boy, (remember 'Heartache Avenue' and '5705'?) and postage stamps, notably 'Charles and Diana - The Royal Wedding', 'Bermuda Miss World', 'Lake Placid Winter Olympics' and 'Spain 1982 World Cup Football' editions.

More recently, his series of incredibly detailed 'Cat Conundrum' puzzle paintings have enthralled and exasperated thousands of dedicated puzzle-solvers all over the world.

Geoff's younger brother, David, is a well-known and extremely successful comedy playwright, so it was no real surprise when Geoff eventually turned his hand to comedy writing, hence this, the seventh full-length novel featuring the chaotic and accident-prone artist, David Day. The stories follow this dreamy, scatterbrained character as he grows up and eventually gets a real job. Geoff's family and friends wonder if he will one day do likewise.

The Hunt for Granddad's Head

Geoff Tristram

DRAWING
ROOM

The right of Geoff Tristram to be identified as author of this work has been asserted.

First published in 2010 by the Drawing Room Press.

Printed and bound in Great Britain by
CPI Antony Rowe, Chippenham and Eastbourne

ISBN 978 0 9551428 6 4

Cover illustration "David, Mr Slavin and the flattened cricket trophy"

by Geoff Tristram.

Contact the author on gt@geofftristram.co.uk

With sincere thanks, as usual, to the incredibly clever Aileen Fraser for editing my books and never once sending me an invoice!

Having written six books about David Day, I was just about to give it a rest. You can have too much of a good thing, I always say. Then, just when I'd resigned myself to the thought of my favourite creation retiring gracefully, an idea popped into my head for a *prequel*. They're all the rage nowadays, apparently, and I didn't want to be left out.

'A Nasty Bump on the Head', my first-ever attempt at writing a novel, has sold very well and is still ticking over nicely, so I thought it would be a great idea to write a book about David in the spring of nineteen-sixty-five, just before 'A Nasty Bump', which began on the sixth of November that same year. The book was what a film company would probably label a PG - suitable for children aged twelve and over, I would have said. Sadly, in a way, but inevitably, the themes of the books became more adult in nature and less suitable for younger children as David got older – he's forty-eight years old in David's Michelangelo, for goodness sake! To make amends, I wanted *this* book to return to that PG rating. It's a book for adults *and* children. A great skill, if you can pull it off!

To fully appreciate this latest story of mine, you must first understand these three things: firstly, children in the nineteen-sixties were quite different from the children of today. They stayed young longer and were *far* more naïve. Secondly, Brierley Bank, the imaginary town where this story is set, was a simple, working class place. David Day lived on a council estate where houses with televisions were quite rare, and houses with phones virtually non-existent. Cheese came in two forms – sharp or mild. And thirdly, no one had ever heard of garlic.

Geoff Tristram

v

Dedicated to the Davids and Garys of this world.

The meek shall eventually inherit the earth,
but probably only after all the others have ruined it for us.

CHAPTER 1

Mike's Legs

Brierley Bank. Spring 1965

Ten-year-old David Day was gluing Mike Summerbee's legs into his football boots when his mother called him in for dinner.

"I can't let go just yet!" he explained to his long-suffering parent, as she dished up his fish fingers. "Otherwise he'll flop backwards again and be stuck there, just like the goalkeeper did yesterday. He looks as if he's limbo-dancing now instead of saving the ball. I'll have to break his legs and start again."

Ruby Day looked heavenwards but only got as far as the polystyrene ceiling tiles. The day that one of her scatterbrained son's sentences actually made some sense would be the time to get *really* worried. She'd become quite used to his hare-brained projects, his flights of fancy, his day-dreaming and his indecipherable thought processes now, and to a loving mother they seemed almost normal. The real time to show concern was when he said something she could

1

more-or-less understand. Then she'd know he was delirious with the fever, or worse.

Against her better judgment, she probed further.

"Who is Mike Summerbee anyway, and why do you need to glue his boots on?"

David gave his mother an exasperated 'women don't know anything' kind of look, omitting to mention that, less than an hour previously, he had similarly been in the dark.

"He's a striker and he's just signed for Manchester City, actually."

"Well why don't you introduce us? And what's he doing in our living room?"

"Very funny, Mother. I'm just mending the Subbuteo team that Trevor Jones swapped me for my microscope. Some of the players have got injuries so I'm gluing their legs back onto their bases."

Ruby Day placed the dinner plate on the kitchen table and insisted he sat down before the food got cold. Sighing heavily, David carefully carried his box of players from the living room into the kitchen and placed them next to his dinner, so that he could keep an eye on Summerbee's condition. It was during another of his mother's unnecessary interruptions that his goalie had flopped over and set solid, and he didn't want his number nine to suffer the same fate. If she carried on this way, he'd end up with a whole team of comatose players, and he'd be the laughing stock of the school. Mike was still looking decidedly wobbly, with huge dollops of glue around his ankles, so David wisely propped him up against his glass of milk for a bit of support while he reluctantly concentrated on the fish fingers. As he ate, he would occasionally rest his head on the Formica work-surface in order to study his tiny team members close-up and from a variety of angles, the better to admire their finely sculpted features. Ruby peered into the tatty cardboard presentation box and frowned.

"And this is what you swapped for that very expensive microscope that your dad got you from work?"

"Yes. It's Manchester City. That's the team I support, you see."

Ruby took a closer look. "You're right. They do appear to have a few injury problems, don't they? There's only four of them who haven't got broken legs. That bloke's got an arm missing, and this one here doesn't have a head. He wouldn't be much good at headers would he?"

"His name is Mike Doyle, and he has got a head, actually," replied David. "Here it is."

He showed his mother the tiny, blond-haired head - no bigger than the head of a match – before carefully placing it back in the box for safe keeping.

"That's my next job after Mike Summerbee's legs."

"This friend of yours – Trevor - he didn't *sit* on this box before he swapped it for the microscope did he?" asked Ruby. "When your dad finds out, he's bound to moan at you. You know he loves to get you interesting toys and things, and you always seem to either paint them a different colour, lose them, wreck them or else swap them for things that the council tip refuse to take. If we'd known you liked Subbuteo, we'd have got you a new team. You haven't mentioned it before, and you don't even have a pitch to play on do you?"

"Ah!" smiled David nervously. "Do you remember that magic set that I never played with?"

Ruby began to study the polystyrene tiles again. "Let me guess. It's magically turned itself into a piece of threadbare green cloth and two goalposts."

"Er, yes."

"And when's this Trevor coming round to take the settee away?"

"Very funny!"

"I wouldn't mind, but since when did you like football?"

David protested in the strongest possible terms. "I *do* like it; it's just that I'm not much good at it. When we play at school, they get you to line up against the wall and the two captains pick a person each. They always leave me till almost last, and I feel embarrassed and stupid. Even when it's my ball they won't pick me, unless I say I'm going home, and then I might get picked, but only if nobody else has got a ball. If it wasn't for Gary Leyton, I reckon they'd pick me last. That's why I got these. I thought I might be better at this than the real thing. I couldn't be any worse, that's for sure! Everybody at school is getting Subbuteo now, and they're trying to organize a proper league, so that each week we can visit each other's houses and play the fixtures. There's going to be a league table and a cup and everything, and I want to be in it. That's why I asked Trevor if I could swap the microscope and my magic set for his old team and

4

pitch. His uncle Jack got him a new Liverpool one for his birthday."

"I see," said Ruby. "Now I suppose he'll be able to tell which player's which, with the help of his new microscope. And who's Gary, this lad who's even worse at football than you?"

"He's my friend," explained David. "Gary is no good at sport because there's something wrong with his leg, and he walks funny. Mally Lobes said that when he was a toddler, he ate a poisoned Polo mint and it made his leg go wonky."

Ruby stared at her boy incredulously. He was at it again, with his bizarre ramblings. Then, suddenly, she began to laugh out loud, once the penny had dropped.

"You mean *polio*. The poor child! It's a horrible disease that can affect children's limbs. Do you remember that sugar lump you had to take recently with medicine in it? You know – the only occasion when the nurse came to the school that you didn't go white and faint – well that was to try and prevent it. What a shame! Does he get upset about it?"

"Yes," said David, "especially when the rough kids call him nasty names, like spastic and cripple because he's got a metal rod thing supporting his leg and he sort of drags his leg around behind him. Sometimes they make him cry in the playground."

"I hope *you* don't ever call him names, David," said Ruby sternly, knowing full well that it wasn't in his nature.

"Of course not," he assured her. "Gary is my friend, because we both like the same things. You know - drawing and playing the recorder and writing stories and so on. He's friends with Mally Lobes as well, and we're both kind to him and sort of apologize when Brett Spittle calls him a name, even though it's not our fault."

Ruby smiled proudly at her son. For all his faults, which were many and varied, he was a gentle, artistic soul. It was nice to hear that his other friend, Mally, though not what one would describe as gentle or artistic, was equally concerned about Gary's condition. Anyway, with huge ears like his, she mused, he could hardly tease other pupils about their physical shortcomings.

David examined Mike Summerbee with a worried look. While they had been talking, the striker's body had slumped forwards, as if someone had kicked him in the shorts. There was an audible click when David tried to rectify his posture, indicating that rigor mortis had already set in.

"And why on earth did you buy Manchester City?" asked Ruby, nonplussed. "Why not a local team, like the Albion or Wolves, or the Villa perhaps?"

"Robert Glazier's bagged the Villa, Peter Fisher's bagged Wolves and Mally has bagged Albion. *Everybody* wanted Manchester United, so just to be different, I went for Manchester City, and anyway, I liked their strip. Sky blue with little claret rings round the socks. All I've got to do now is save up for the away strip, which is red and black stripes."

"You could always tell Trevor about Jennings," suggested Ruby. "Perhaps he'd consider swapping his away team for your hamster, to save me and your dad having to clean it out every week."

6

David was horrified. "I am *not* swapping my hamster!" he insisted, his lip quivering. "I promise I'll clean the cage from now on, honest. I don't want to swap my hamster!"

"Relax!" smiled Ruby. "I was joking. Don't get worked up. Mind you, I wasn't joking about cleaning the cage. It stinks, and it's not fair on the little thing that lives in it either. You'd better get back to school now, before the bell goes, but I want it cleaned out tonight, and no excuses, or Trevor gets him."

David promised faithfully to do his duty, and headed for the outhouse door.

"You've spent far too long mucking around with your footballers' legs this dinner time," said Ruby, removing her pinafore. "You'd best go on your bike now, or you'll be late."

"Ah!" replied David cryptically, before running like the wind in the direction of Brierley Bank Junior School, his brand new satchel dragging along on the tarmac behind him.

CHAPTER 2

An ill wind

First lesson on Monday morning was double art – David's favourite. He may have been hopeless at sports, largely due to being constructed pretty much along the lines of an undernourished stick-insect, but when it came to art, he was in a league of his own. So prodigious was he that, in spite of his tender years, not one of his teachers could compete with him. If Miss Dukes needed a drawing of a Triceratops in a hurry, or Mr Perriman was desirous of a skeleton to better illustrate his biology lesson, David was summoned with his paints, his pencils and his thirteen-colour biro to save the day. It was even mooted by David's form teacher, the kindly Mr Lewis, that the lad should really be sent to the nearby secondary school for specialist lessons under the tutelage of a real art teacher, rather than a primary school 'jack of all trades' such as himself. Given that Mr Lewis had the artistic skills of the average four-year-old, this wasn't such a bad idea.

"I'm sorry, David," the Welshman would say, "I can't even draw a straight line without a ruler!"

"No-one can," David would assure him, desperately trying to stifle a giggle at his favourite teacher's attempts to illustrate a point on the blackboard. "That's what rulers were invented for, sir."

"Fair enough, but when I try to draw a dog, it always comes out looking like a cross between a blasted budgerigar and an octopus. I'm hopeless! Do you remember the horse I drew last week in biology?"

The entire class began to snigger.

"The trouble is, sir," continued David, pleased to be the centre of attention, "you don't seem to have a good memory for how things are constructed. Horse's legs bend a different way to human legs for a start."

"They do?"

"Yes, sir, and do you remember your famous frog drawing? Frogs have got *four* limbs, I think you'll find."

"Well I never! I knew something looked odd about it."

The children had been looking forward to the day's art class for some time, as their inept form teacher had promised to take them up to Brierley Bank Church to draw in the graveyard. The venue itself wasn't particularly setting them alight, but any excursion that took them out of the school's front gates was regarded as infinitely preferable to normal lessons. For those who didn't fancy the slightly macabre subject matter, he'd also managed to organize a brass-rubbing session inside the church, courtesy of the new vicar, the Reverend George McKenzie.

David, in particular, was excited about the trip, because it gave him a chance to shine. School Sports Day would see him limping home fifteenth in the egg and spoon race, just in front of Fatty Foley, or gasping for breath and dropping his baton in the four-hundred-yard relay, much to the amusement of his peers. Today, however, they would be gathered around, marvelling at how he coped with the church's complex perspective, and hanging on his every word as he explained how he achieved light, shade and texture. Nor would this adulation be reserved for his classmates. Mr Lewis too would stand over his little pocket-sized John Constable and gaze down with pride and wonder, only to be interrupted by the inevitable sea of raised hands.

"Sir, sir! How do you draw a tree, sir?"

"Ask David, Edward!"

Sir, sir! I can't get this roof right."

"Ask David, Sarah, ask David!"

David, of course, protested that the constant barrage of questions was interrupting his flow, but secretly he loved every minute of the attention he received. It made up for the humiliation he suffered on the playing fields.

Mr Lewis asked his pupils to put on their coats and hats, and collect a drawing board from over by the sink. Then he invited them to follow him, in single-file and without chattering, out of the classroom, down the long corridor and out into the big wide world - if Brierley Bank could ever be described as big or wide. In fact, it was just the opposite – small and narrow. The small Black Country town was built on a very steep hill, with the junior school near to the bottom. The children stood at the crossings, and waited for their teacher to stride into the middle of the road to halt the traffic. Usually, this rather foolhardy act was performed with consummate ease and authority by Barbara, the roly-poly crossing lady, but she had returned home following her morning shift.

Barbara, unlike Mr Lewis, did not fear the traffic, presumably because she was built roughly along the lines of a Sherman tank and could bat away any troublesome vehicles with a flick of her huge arms, if they got too close. Though only five-feet tall, she had a body eminently suited to all-in wrestling, and could legitimately claim to be the only crossing lady who was actually taller lying on her back than standing up. The other advantage she had over the athletic-looking Mr Lewis was that, if a car did succeed in colliding with her, the amount of natural padding she possessed – mainly in her colossal arms and impressive chest – would ensure that the damage to both parties would be minimal.

Crossing himself theatrically like a Roman Catholic priest and then bouncing into action, the brave Welshman eventually persuaded Brierley Bank's drivers to rest awhile, after a near miss with a myopic octogenarian on a moped. Having chivvied the boisterous human crocodile safely across the road, he led them up the steep hill towards the church, which was conveniently situated right at the other end of the high street.

Anyone who was not familiar with the town would have deduced that it was entirely inhabited by carnivorous alcoholics with a penchant for knitwear; such was the number of pubs, butchers' shops and wool emporia. This would not, in fairness, have painted the whole picture, however. On closer inspection, Brierley Bankers also seemed fond of coal, hardware and haircuts. David cringed as he passed Freddie Fielding's Barber shop, the scene of many a vicious and unnecessary scalping.

Freddie had an unfortunate knack of being able to recreate Adolf Hitler's exact hairstyle, and he seemed intent on spreading the gospel, so that virtually everyone who lived in Brierley Bank was encouraged to sport one, or go without a haircut altogether. The problem was caused by the fact that, whilst there were several ladies' salons, competition for men's barbershops was non-existent, unless one travelled to Cradley Heath, the next town along. Even then, the choice was hardly worth the bus-fare, with only the 'Stan Laurel' or the 'Oliver Hardy' on offer. Had Hitler succeeded in invading and conquering Britain, one could only speculate as to what he would have made of Brierley Bank. Presumably, he would have been pleased. On the other hand, perhaps his home-town in Austria was plagued by a plethora of severe barbers, and the style he sported was not of his own choice. This may even have been the reason why he had become so bitter and twisted in later life.

After the barber shop came several assorted butchers' shops, and towards the centre of the high street, on the other side of the road, there stood the formidable Miss Kettle's Toy and Joke Emporium. Whereas Freddie Fielding was a fundamentally decent man handicapped by a limited range of both hairstyles and conversation – namely the 'Hitler', the 'Hitler Youth' and West Bromwich Albion – Miss Kettle was another kettle of fish altogether. The woman was an ogre. She hated children - and adults, for that matter - with a vengeance. Her opinion of cats and dogs has not been put on record, but one presumes that anything that lived and breathed was equally unwelcome in her shop. The reason that Brierley Bank children tended to *swap* their meagre possessions was almost certainly due to her. They were simply too terrified to enter her domain in order to buy new things, even if they had the money.

After passing a few more butchers' shops, pubs and a wool shop, Mr Lewis led his charges into the churchyard, and was glad to have remembered his gloves and hat. A biting wind had gathered momentum, and the temperature had dipped considerably.

The brass-rubbers, mainly girls, followed him into church to meet the new vicar, whilst the hardened and dedicated churchyard sketchers set up their work stations outside. David, Mally and Gary chose a spot under a big old birch tree, next to a weathered Victorian urn mounted on a large stone plinth, inscribed with the words:

Jeremiah Silversmith 1821 -1899

- Carpenter -

Lived alone, worked alone and died alone.

Now in God's care forevermore.

"He sounded like a cheerful soul," said Mally, frowning and scratching his head.

"I don't know why we have to draw here anyway," moaned Gary, rubbing his hands together vigorously. "Couldn't we have gone somewhere a bit less depressing, like a murder scene or something?"

"I quite like it, actually," said David, busily fastening his cartridge paper to his board with drawing pins. "As long as we don't have to come here at night of course! My advice is to draw the church, not the graves. It's a bit more cheerful."

"It might be more cheerful, but it's flippin' harder to draw," moaned Mally. He was a country boy at heart, and could manage a half-decent pheasant or a trout from memory, but hated architectural stuff.

Brett Spittle slouched over to where the three had set up base camp and wasted no time in being unpleasant, an attitude for which his face was eminently suited.

"I knew I'd find the three girls together," he began. "Arty Farty, Big Ears and the Spaz. Teacher's pets!"

The pug-faced, slit-eyed little monster's insults were a little too obvious for David's taste. If he was to be insulted at all – and he'd much rather not have been - he preferred something with a bit more panache, and was himself capable of extremely biting sarcasm, a skill he inherited from his father's side of the family. He did tend to temper this a little during school hours, however, due to his lack of the essential pugilistic skills he needed to back it up, if all else failed.

Thankfully, Mr Lewis arrived just in time to prevent further nastiness, and directed the repellent Spittle to the far end of the graveyard, no doubt secretly wishing that the boy could have been a permanent resident. Mr Lewis tried hard to see the best in everyone, but with Spittle, it was asking a lot. The problem was, he came from a rough part of town, and his parents were the type who had hated school themselves, and encouraged their offspring to do likewise. If it had been legal to drag a child out of school at seven and send him up a chimney, they would have been pleased to do so. Because of this, everything that Mr Lewis tried to do at school was instantly undone when the boy got home. Some days, the teacher felt as if he were banging his head against a brick wall. Then, just as he would be fantasizing about early retirement and a spot of fishing back home in the Elan Valley, Gary Leyton would present him with a nice bit of calligraphy, or David Day would paint him a magnificent picture. Occasionally, in his more rational moments, Dai Lewis could see that Brett Spittle was not entirely to blame for his actions. It was his parents who were guilty, and their parents before them, probably. If Mr Lewis himself had been raised to think that kicking the bull terrier was perfectly acceptable from birth, would *he* have known any different? Were people inherently bad, or just encouraged to be that way early on in their lives? It was all very well trying to educate children at school, but they could often become de-educated again the second they got home, depending on which influence was the stronger. Taking that to its logical conclusion, maybe it was the *parents* of murderers and criminals who should be standing in the dock, alongside, or even instead of, their odious offspring. It made sense, in a way, but the only trouble with that was, how far back would the judge allow one to trawl? 'I'm sorry I was drunk, disorderly and ginger-haired, Your Honour, but I blame my Viking ancestors.' Somehow, Mr Lewis couldn't see that working in a court of law. No, Brett Spittle was a little swine, whichever way he looked at it. Even his name was revolting, and the teacher did at least feel confident in blaming the parents for that, if nothing else.

Feeling that he was virtually redundant in terms of artistic tuition, Mr Lewis mumbled, "I can trust you three, so just get on with it, lads," and strolled off to get a cup of tea and a biscuit with the vicar, hoping against hope that Brett and his band of cut-throat mercenaries weren't planning to desecrate an ancient grave or behead the daffodils.

David, meanwhile, had set off at a blistering pace, sketching furiously and humming a jaunty tune.

"I'm flipping freezing," complained Gary, rubbing his bad leg to get some feeling back into it. "I thought this was supposed to be springtime!"

"It's the mad March winds, but they're late, because it's April," explained Mally, who knew about nature. "Did you hear that then? It's actually howling."

"Sounds spooky to me," said David, blowing into his hands, "especially here, in a church yard, of all places."

Suddenly, the wind swirled violently into the foliage above them, causing the boys to leap up from the cold grass, startled. The gust was followed immediately by a loud cracking noise, which saw Mally and David vacating the area beneath the tree as fast as their legs would carry them, and Gary endeavouring to do likewise - the drawing boards, pencils and erasers abandoned in blind panic.

Then, dramatically, a huge branch of the old birch tree sheered off, creaking horribly, and smashed down onto the old urn above the plinth. The lichen-encrusted urn shattered upon impact and fell onto the grass in twenty or more jagged pieces. Once the drama was over, the three boys nervously stepped forward to examine the remains, keeping a weather eye on the tree above them as they did so. On the floor, partially obscured by the stone shards, lay an old, yellowed envelope. It had brown writing on the front – the kind David had seen before, in his calligraphy book. It read:

To whom it may concern.

"Oh well," said David, picking it up. "I suppose it concerns us now!"

The Reverend McKenzie and Mr Lewis had heard the commotion, and were running towards the accident scene with worried looks on their faces.

"Is anyone hurt?" called the teacher, panicking somewhat.

"No, sir!" Mally called back, "But the gravestone is wrecked, and we've found this letter!"

"Let me take a look," said Mr Lewis.

Meanwhile, the Reverend was doing his best to scrape together the bits of urn and place them next to the plinth, 'tut tutting' wearily as he did so. Mr Lewis carefully opened the old envelope and removed a stained letter from within. He read it out loud to those present.

"My name is, or should I say was, Jeremiah. I daresay that I have long since been forgotten, and this would hardly surprise me, as I wasn't held in great affection while I was alive either.

I was brought up by a father who enjoyed beating me and a mother who was too drunk to take notice. For this reason, I decided to take my leave of them as soon as it was possible. I had no brothers or sisters, and so I became something of a recluse, I'm afraid. I have never known affection, and perhaps because of this, I have been unable to show any to others. Instead, I spent my waking hours working by myself, learning my trade and only relying on other people for my materials and provisions. Because I did not have a wife and children, or a solitary friend in this world, other than my books, I also did not have to endure the distractions that encumber other folk. Hence, I was able to work more diligently and for longer hours than most are wont to do, and by doing so, earn a substantial amount of money.

The only problem with this was that I also had no real inclination to spend it. I was not in the least gregarious, nor did I smoke or drink, so when the physician informed me that my tedious, solitary life was coming to an end, for which, incidentally, I praise God, this raised the vexed question of what I should do with my fortune.

Not having a charity that I felt inclined to donate to, a close friend or even a distant living relative, I have decided upon a course of action that may surprise you. Having been for all of my life a careful, serious, and some would say miserly soul, in death I wish to become mischievous and flippant. I foolishly accumulated my wealth, not realizing that money was only of use if one spent it. I know this now, but alas, the knowledge has come too late. It is interesting how one suddenly understands the meaning of life when one is about to be robbed of it.

I have, therefore, decided to hide my fortune, and I hope whoever finds it makes more use of it than I. I trust you will forgive me for dipping into it in order to pay the feckless and drunken stonemason whom I have foolishly entrusted to create my final resting place. There was little choice in this God-forsaken town, so I hope and pray that he gave me something worth the money I paid. I also hope that my money-grabbing solicitor carried out my instructions to the letter. I presume he did, or else you would not be reading this letter.

I will never know how long it has taken for my secret to come to light. Are you mere nineteenth century grave-robbers or a civilization far more advanced than my own, thousands of years in the future? Am I ancient now, and studied in the same way that archaeologists from my time study the tombs of Egypt, or was I still fresh in the ground? Indeed, would the riches I have hidden still be valued by your new society? If they are not, then how ironic this last act of defiance has been.

Finally, you will be wanting to know how my fortune can be found, so I will tell you. You must look to my trade, and there lies your answer. Seek out my life's work, and there is your reward. I hope that it gives you more pleasure than it ever gave me.

Jeremiah. 1899.

Mr Lewis folded the letter and placed it back in it's envelope with a heavy sigh.

"Well," he said eventually, "that has to be the saddest thing I've heard for a long time."

"I don't quite know what to say," added the vicar. "How tragic! I just hope and pray that the poor man has found friendship and comfort in heaven."

"If there is one," Gary whispered to David.

"Do you doubt it, my friend?" asked the sharp-eared vicar, concerned by the boy's comment.

Mr Lewis gave Gary the sort of look that parents give to a child that has just silently broken wind in the cake shop.

"Sorry, sir," Gary continued, "but God is just a nice story that we get taught at school, just like Father Christmas, but I don't believe in all that now that I'm eleven."

The Reverend McKenzie smiled a sad smile.

"You mustn't confuse the two stories, son. Father Christmas *is* a made-up story for young children, as you now know."

"It is?" asked David, visibly shattered.

"No, no, I, erm, I mean…" The vicar's face turned a bright crimson, and he was floundering terribly. "This isn't a conversation I want to get into really," he blustered. "What I meant was…"

"It's okay, I'm teasing," smiled David. I've known since last Christmas, but I was very upset when I found out."

Mally bit his lip and tried to look brave. He'd just heard some rather distressing news.

"What I'm trying to say is that Father Christmas is a lovely thing for children to believe in, but there comes a time when they need to grow up and accept that it is nothing more than a story, whereas God is real, and grown-ups believe in Him."

"So God is a sort of Father Christmas for grown-ups?" asked Gary.

Mr Lewis shuffled from foot to foot. It was not like the mild-mannered Gary Leyton to be so probing. The vicar tried to continue, but Gary had got the bit between his teeth now.

"I can't see the difference. They're both fairy stories. Father Christmas couldn't possibly get round to all those children in one night, and if he drank all those glasses of sherry, he'd be drunk. When you're little, you believe all sorts of rubbish, because you don't realize how daft it is. It's like God making the world and the animals in seven days, and Jesus waking up again after he'd been crucified, and the loaves and fishes thing. Now I'm eleven, I don't believe it anymore."

"But..." said the vicar.

"And if there's a God, why did he punish me by giving me polio and making my leg wonky, when I'd done nothing wrong?"

"Well..."

"God doesn't look after everyone on this planet. He hasn't got the time, just like Father Christmas can't visit every child in one night. It's just a silly story."

"Perhaps he's like Doctor Who," suggested Mally, still struggling to come to terms with the Father Christmas bombshell.

"Lads, I think we need to find another area to draw in," interjected Mr Lewis, eager to change the subject, "and leave the vicar to try and sort out this mess."

"Who's like Doctor Who?" asked Gary, "God or Father Christmas?"

"Well, I actually meant Father Christmas," explained Mally, desperately trying to hang on to his childhood. "Maybe he can travel through time and space and be in lots of places all at once. Then Father Christmas *could* exist, couldn't he, Reverend McKenzie?"

"Not really," sighed the vicar, wishing he'd never started the debate in the first place. "I would say that was impossible."

"Well, if I want to believe in it, I can, can't I?" asked Mally.

"And if I want to believe in God, then I can!" smiled the vicar.

"How do we stand on the tooth fairy?" asked Mr Lewis, ruffling his hair in an exasperated way.

"You can both believe in whatever you like," frowned Gary, "but that doesn't mean you're right."

"Lads, lads, we need to get on with our art lesson," insisted Mr Lewis. "And Gary, can you have a little respect for your elders, please? We've all had a bit of a shock, and you're getting a bit over-excited now. Gather up your stuff and follow me; there's a nice spot over there without any trees, and we've accomplished nothing yet." Absent-mindedly, he pocketed the letter, ushering the boys away, so that the shaken reverend could clean up.

A few minutes later, the boys were drawing again, but it was understandably difficult to push the earlier dramatic events to the backs of their minds, especially with the fascinating prospect of discovering hidden treasure.

"That letter belongs to us," protested Mally indignantly. "Sir's nicked it so that he can find the money."

"He wouldn't do that," insisted David, who had a soft spot for his teacher. "I'm sure he'll let us read it again at school. Besides, it didn't say much. Just that it was something to do with his work, I think. We'd have to find out who the man was first, and what he did for a job. I suppose they'd have records of it somewhere."

"He was a carpenter, remember?" said Gary. "It said so on that gravestone thing. Maybe there's a list of carpenters in Brierley Bank somewhere. My dad is in the local history society. I bet he'd know!"

"Right!" piped up David, "You can ask him tonight. If I were you, I'd keep this secret, just between ourselves – the three musketeers!

Meanwhile, at the other end of the churchyard, a middle-aged gentleman sporting a big, bushy white beard and clad in an old red duffel coat, had been on his hands and knees collecting the many broken pieces of stone and placing them in an old coal sack. He stood up unsteadily, groaning as his arthritic knees creaked beneath him.

Father McKenzie brushed off the dirt from his hands as he walked from the grave, back up the stone path to his church. He needed a strong cup of tea, more than anything on earth. Why was it, he wondered, that he could hold a congregation of adults spellbound in the palm of his hands, yet these three eleven-year-olds had flummoxed him completely.

CHAPTER 3

Witch Hazel

"Mom," said David, as he carried Jennings's home into the living room, "can we get a television?"

"Your dad keeps on about one too," replied Ruby, "so maybe we'll think about it soon. Have many of your friends got one, then?"

"A few have and a lot still haven't. I really want one. Even Brett Spittle's got one, and his family live in a dirty old house with junk in the garden."

Ruby gave him one of her looks. "Oh, that's right, David. Make us feel guilty because we haven't got a telly yet. You'll be after a telephone next!"

"Don't be silly!" smiled David. "Nobody I know has got one of those! Nobody on our estate anyway. I bet footballers and millionaires have got 'em though, and tellys as well."

"Well, your dad isn't a footballer, or a millionaire, and I doubt whether he'll ever be well off, making machine tools for a living. We're much better off than a lot of people in Brierley Bank though, so be grateful. Lord knows how that

Mrs Spittle can afford a telly. Probably stole it, knowing them!"

Ruby Day was not one of Edith Spittle's biggest fans, it was fair to say. The loud-mouthed and abrasive woman would blindly defend her son, Brett, even when it was patently obvious to just about everyone in Brierley Bank that he was a little monster. When he had tried to shove David into the 'Nine Locks' canal basin because he wouldn't hand over his conkers, Ruby had sought out Mrs Spittle in the High Street in order to make her feelings clear, but had backed off when the lady became overly aggressive. Ruby, though mild-mannered, could not let an injustice go by unchallenged, but she had been shocked by both Mrs Spittle's colourful language and her blinkered denial that darling Brett could have done such a thing.

"Your boy must have started it," she snarled. "My Brett would never do that without a reason, and that's if he did it at all. You're a bloody liar, Mrs Day, and so is your son. It was probably him that bullied our Brett, and he was just defending himself, the way his dad taught him."

Brett Spittle had an ingenious way of defending himself, it had to be said. Rather than wait until some perceived slight had actually occurred, or a hand was raised, he would wade in and begin thumping and kicking, just to be on the safe side. Brett liked to get his retaliation in first. He had left a bloody trail caused by his premature self-defence tactics all over town – and his 'assailants' were nearly always considerably smaller or less able than himself. Many of the angry parents deemed it necessary to bite their lips and say nothing, just in case their complaints escalated the problem, but Ruby Day was too full of righteous indignation to do likewise. After five minutes with Mrs Spittle, she was wishing she'd followed the advice of other parents. She had also unwittingly made David's predicament worse. Edith would probably return home after the confrontation and request that her darling Brett gave David a good kicking at the earliest available opportunity, just to remind Mrs Day to button her lip the next time their paths crossed in town.

* * *

David carefully placed his hamster's lavish residence onto the previous night's Express and Star newspaper and removed the roof grill.

Jenning's home was a cut above the average hamster cage, thanks to Len Day, David's dad. Len was the foreman in a tool-making shop at a factory in Cradley Heath, and an incurable perfectionist. If he made something, whether it be in wood or metal, it would be 'just so', no matter how humble the item or its purpose. Jennings's cage was a split-level accommodation with a choice of two bedrooms and an open-plan living room – the sort of bachelor pad that other rodents could only dream of. Mod cons included an end-to-end picture window, giving a panoramic view of Len's tool shed, a fully equipped gymnasium (exercise wheel and see-saw) and a deluxe mahogany dining table with porcelain seed and water troughs either side. If Len had had more time, he would probably have installed central heating too.

David helped his placid pet out of its quarters and placed him on the carpet, while he set about the clean-up operation. He sprinkled a few seeds onto the nearby Subbuteo pitch, just in case Jennings became peckish, and left him to it.

"Look," laughed Ruby, breaking off from her endless ironing. "Jennings fancies himself as a footballer!"

The cute little creature was weaving in and out of David's crippled Manchester City players, and nudging the ball with his nose. After tiring of this, he began exploring the immediate vicinity in search of seed, which he began to shovel into his cheek pouches at an alarming rate.

Ten minutes later, the hamster house cleaned after a fashion, Jenning's freedom was brought to an abrupt end, and he was incarcerated once more.

"Oh, flipping marvellous!" sighed his notoriously squeamish owner, as he surveyed the landscape. He's pooed all over my pitch, and done another couple in my Manchester City Subbuteo box. Charming!"

"Well clean it up," replied Ruby. "You don't want Mike Summerbeetle stepping in it – or the headless chap. He can't see where he's going."

"Ha ha!"

"And if I were you, I'd give Jennings enough food and water to last the weekend, because we're going to the caravan. And I bet blooming Edith Spittle and her husband haven't got one of *those*!"

David greeted this latest announcement with enthusiasm. A few years previously, his grandparents, Bertha and Reuben, had invested in a caravan near Tenbury Wells in Worcestershire, so that the family could have a change of scenery at weekends and during holidays. Bertha and Reuben couldn't drive, and Ruby and Len couldn't afford a caravan, so it was an arrangement that suited both parties.

The site was a small, rural place next to an old country pub, and David loved it. He may have been a town boy on weekdays, but come Friday night, he could escape to the country and live a completely different type of life until Sunday teatime. Tenbury meant a chance to explore endless woods, observe the abundant wildlife, go fishing by the Teme and draw pictures in his sketchbooks by the light of a cosy gas mantle, if it was raining. His family also enjoyed the country life, which, for them, centred around The Olde Inn next to the site. The pub was populated by caravanners from the Black Country and local rustic types who never seemed to use currency to buy drinks, instead favouring the bartering system. The former, having no dead rabbits, pheasants or vegetables to exchange, parted willingly with their hard-earned cash in return for indescribably potent home-brewed cider, or for the less foolhardy, Banks's Mild.

This rural idyll was almost paradise on earth as far as David was concerned, with one small reservation. He needed company of his own age. Admittedly, there were local children to play with, or the offspring of his fellow caravanners, but their presence could never be guaranteed. Some weekends, he might be the only child on the site, and this deflated him somewhat. Exploring, fishing and having adventures was great fun, but it was infinitely better with two. Had he only realized how brothers and sisters were created, he would not have wasted time in putting in a request to his parents. Still lacking this vital piece of biological knowledge, he kept his desire for a brother or sister to himself, for the time being. Instead, he resolved to broach the subject of taking a playmate at the next possible opportunity, which came sooner than he had expected.

Usually, the caravan would be full, by the time that Bertha, Reuben, Ruby, Len and David had claimed their sleeping quarters. This weekend, however, David's grandparents had elected to give it a miss, as Reuben wished to support the team he used to play for, Brierley Bank Celtic F.C., in their home tie against Dudley Town. The game was a first round match in the Dudley League Knockout Cup, and the fixtures were always hotly contested. Due to the awkward timing of this particular premier sporting fixture, the caravan had spare capacity, and David's timely request to take a school friend was treated sympathetically.

"Who would you take, *if* we let you?" asked Ruby, once Jennings had been returned to the shed. She stressed the 'if', just in case David nominated some unspeakable thug or irritating little tyke that she didn't care for. Two rainy days in a small caravan could get very claustrophobic with the wrong child in tow.

"Mally Lobes or Gary, probably," replied David, with his fingers crossed.

"Choose," suggested Ruby. "They might not be allowed to go anyway, remember, so don't get your hopes up yet."

"Okay, Gary then. He needs cheering up, I think," said David after much pondering.

"Is that the lad with polio?"

"Yes. I could take him fishing, and perhaps dad might take us to the Regal on Saturday to watch a film. It'll make up for us not having a telly."

"Rub it in, why don't you?" asked Ruby. "I'll see what your dad says when he gets home from work. He'll probably say yes, as long as you assure me that this lad's nice and polite. It'll save us having to entertain you."

"Thank you, mom!" grinned David, thrilled to bits. "He is *very* polite. Unless you're a vicar!"

Ruby seldom expected her son's comments to make sense, and on this occasion she was not disappointed. She briefly toyed with the notion of asking David to explain himself, but decided against it at the last second because she knew full well the explanation would probably be just as unfathomable as his initial comment had been. Instead, she merely asked her son to ask Gary to ask his parents if they had any objections to loaning him out for two days, with the proviso that he would be fed, watered and entertained.

After the jungle telegraph had relayed a few garbled messages back and forth, and Mr and Mrs Leyton were assured that David's parents were not devil worshippers with a penchant for sacrificing and devouring children, the deal was done. Gary would be picked up on Friday evening at six, en-route to Tenbury Wells, armed with his pyjamas, toothbrush and ten bob to spend.

* * *

Len's sky-blue Austin Cambridge Shooting Brake pulled alongside Bertha and Reuben's caravan at seven o'clock, and the Day family piled out, followed closely by a very excited Gary Leyton. He had never been in a caravan before, and it all seemed very exotic. David, who was possibly even more excited than his friend, gave Gary the guided tour, pointing out the hidden bed in the wall, the chemical lavatory, the gas fire, the magazine rack and anything else he could think of. Saving the best till last, he showed Gary into the cramped bedroom that was to be theirs for the weekend, with its bunk beds, window, tiny wardrobe and not much else. He proudly extracted the dusty fishing equipment from beneath the bed, but tactfully left the case-ball and cricket stumps in the wardrobe, realizing that Gary was not the greatest sportsman. After tossing a threepenny bit for the top bunk, which Gary won, they unpacked their meagre belongings and settled down with an Eagle comic each until dinner was ready.

After a simple but hearty meal of beef stew with dumplings and pearl barley, followed by apple pie and custard, the boys decided to explore the caravan park while Ruby washed up and Len fiddled manfully with his dipstick. The first thing that struck Gary, almost literally, was the thrilling air display which was laid on especially, courtesy of the site's bats. He'd never seen bats before, and now he was seeing hundreds of them. They dive-bombed him as he walked down the main driveway with David, missing his head by inches and causing him to duck.

"You get used to them after a while," David assured him. "They never hit you. Granny Bertha's scared of them, because she thinks they get tangled up in your hair. She's so funny! She hides in the pantry when there's thunder, and when she's in dad's car and another car is trying to pass in the narrow country lanes, she gets me to move across in my seat to make more room! When she gets tiddly in The Olde Inn, she gets up on the pub tables and sings 'Ramona', and all the farmers cheer."

"I'm not bothered about these bats," Gary assured him, "but I hate fat moths."

"So do I!" agreed David, shuddering at the thought. "You get loads of 'em round here as well, so we have to be careful not to open the caravan door when the gas lights are on. I'm scared of wasps most of all though. Last year, we were down here and this local kid asked me to help him get rid of a wasp nest just over there. He fetched a kettle of boiling water and poured it down the hole, and seconds later, this mad swarm came out and attacked us. We went running down the lane at a hundred miles an hour with this black swarm after us, and I got stung on the ear-hole about twenty times or something. I could see them all swarming around my face, taking it in turns. I've been terrified of them ever since."

"Funny how we all have different things that we're scared of," mused Gary. "I bet Brett blooming Spittle isn't scared of things though. He just makes the rest of us scared. If I had to make a list, I'd write; Fat Moths, Brett Spittle, Daddy Longlegs and Injections."

"Brett Spittle has to be scared of *something*," replied David, "but he'd never tell us what it was, that's the trouble. My list is: Wasps, Swimming Lessons, Brett Spittle, of course, Injections and the Dentist's Van that comes into the playground. I go all pale and giddy when I talk about that van, just thinking about the horror of it!"

The boys wandered back to the caravan to get changed, so that they could go to the pub with Ruby and Len for an hour. Unlike the pubs in Brierley Bank, which usually confined the children to an awful, brightly lit, dusty room with a squeaky blackboard if they were lucky, and a cold, tiled corridor if they weren't, The Olde Inn allowed them into the lounge if they behaved themselves. It also allowed the odd Border collie, parrot, bird of prey, ferret, pony and sheep in there too, if they did likewise.

After a jolly evening spent playing bar billiards and shove halfpenny, drinking Vimto and scoffing obscene amounts of crisps and pork scratchings, David and Gary were rounded up and told it was time to head home. Tired but happy, they trudged back across the pitch-black field with Ruby and Len, their torches darting this way and that in search of rabbits, until they reached the welcoming door of the caravan. Ruby shone her torch on the keyhole while Len, who had probably had one too many pints of Banks's Mild to perform intricate operations, fumbled with his key-ring for a good ten minutes in an attempt to locate the one with 'Yale' printed on it. Eventually, after much cursing under the breath and childish laughter, the door was opened, and the four entered at speed, closing the door quickly again after them before the fat moths arrived. Once inside, Len asked the boys to aim their torches at the various gas mantles, which he endeavoured to light, with little success, due entirely to the fact that he'd forgotten to turn on the gas bottle outside. The interior of the caravan now resembled a re-enactment of the Battle of Britain, with searchlights zipping all over the place, as ghostly part-illuminated figures stumbled and fell over breakfast tables, magazine racks and stools, much to the boys' amusement. Ten minutes later, however, reason was restored to its throne, and the caravan was once more bathed in poetic gaslight. Children's clothes were thrown in heaps for the clothes-folding fairies to tidy up in time for morning, pyjamas were pulled on and teeth were cleaned, while Len and Ruby lowered the foldaway bed from the wall. It was nearly midnight now, and the boys were on their last legs. Ruby settled them into their bunks, tucked them in and said 'God bless!' before slipping into the double bed at the other end of the caravan. A solitary owl hooted 'goodnight' to them from a nearby tree.

"Dave," whispered Gary, yawning.

"Yeah?"

"I'm having a great time."

"Me too. We'll go exploring tomorrow."

"And fishing, maybe?"

David didn't answer. He was already fast asleep.

* * *

Breakfast tasted better in a caravan. Gary was convinced of this. At home he would hardly touch his toast, but in the caravan he had consumed more food than a transport café full of obese truck drivers could have managed. Len told Gary that he was pleased he had enjoyed it, and he would be welcome to stay again, as long as it was not before the Day household celebrated a sizable win on Littlewoods Pools. The comment flew at least a yard over Gary's head and vanished into the ether, causing David, who was far more attuned to his father's sense of humour, to look at his parent askance.

Once the breakfast things were cleared away, the boys were sent down the path to the building that housed the showers and lavatories, a depressing breeze-block affair full of overly-cheerful men in vests, whistling jaunty tunes as they shaved. Once their ablutions were completed, they returned to the caravan with soggy towels under their arms, and declared that they were to spend the morning exploring.

"Be careful," warned Ruby, as they slipped on their Wellingtons. "Stay together, and don't speak to strangers."

"They're okay down here," smiled Len. "It's not like it was London or some big city. They'll be fine, but don't go trespassing onto farmland or we might be spending tonight tweezering shotgun pellets out of your backsides!"

This did nothing for Ruby's confidence.

"It's all very well saying that Tenbury is safe, Len. Yorkshire was safe till somebody started abducting children last year."

Gary was starting to look worried now.

"Look, there's nothing to worry about. Just don't go far and stay off private land," Len assured them. "And I want you back here by dinner time, because we're off fishing this afternoon."

They headed off to the front gates, and, after much deliberation, turned right, for no apparent reason. After a mile or so of country lane, they saw a public footpath to the left, and took it. The path meandered along the edge of a farmer's field for almost half a mile, before a stile blocked their way. David clambered over it and waited patiently for Gary to do likewise. They were on another country lane now, but this one was narrower, with high hedgerows, and its roughly laid and oft-repaired tarmac was awash with mud and cattle manure. After gingerly stepping through the quagmire, they came across a tiny, dilapidated old cottage with an algae-covered caravan next to it. In the small, open front garden, someone had laid out a rough trestle table with various types of garden produce. A scruffy, hand-painted sign announced 'Garlics for Sale'.

"What a strange old place!" said David. "What's garlic anyway?"

Gary was deep in thought. He *knew* that word. It was in the back of his mind somewhere, but he was struggling to recall where he'd heard it before.

His thought processes were interrupted by a lady of around thirty-five years of age with very long, straggly hair and a floor-length floral skirt which had seen better days. She opened her front door, just as the two boys were studying her table of produce, causing them to leap at least three feet into the air.

"Hello, lads," she said, with a thick, country accent. "My name's Hazel. Can I help you then?"

"Er, no, thank you," stammered David, his heart still pounding. "We were just looking at your things."

"They're all fresh," announced the lady. "I grows 'em in me garden, back there. Anything you need?"

"Not really, my mom and dad get ours from the grocer's shop in Brierley Bank. We're just on holiday."

"Grocer's shop vegetables are no good," snapped the lady, shaking her head. "Full of chemicals, see, to keep 'em fresh. These comes right out the ground and onto your plate, the old-fashioned way. I lives the old way, you see, without modern distractions. No television, no car, no telephone, no clocks."

"It's a wonder you've got a house!" observed Gary tartly. He may have had a gammy leg, but his tongue worked beautifully.

36

"What are those?" he continued, pointing to a couple of white bulbs in a wicker basket. "I've never seen any of those before."

"Ah!" cackled the lady, wiping her filthy hands down her skirt. "Garlics, them am. They has all sorts of mysterious, magical powers. They can kill bacteria, cure diseases, you name it! Garlic can even kill werewolves and vampires. That's how powerful them little things am. "

"So if you've got garlic, there's no need to ever see the doctor?" asked Gary. He was seriously toying with the idea of rubbing one on his leg.

"The doctor?" replied the lady dismissively. "The doctor isn't welcome here, I can tell you. I don't trust him, with his modern medicines that fill you full of chemicals. I prefer the old ways – nature's ways. Me and the doctor are sworn enemies. I don't trust him, and as far as he's concerned I'm from another planet!"

She picked up a small garlic bulb from her basket and broke it open to reveal the cloves within. "See this? There's around twelve little pods inside, and each one of 'em is an incredibly powerful thing, once it's fully grown."

The lady threw a mature, unopened bulb to David.

"You can keep that, being as I like the look of you, but remember, treat it with respect."

"Er, thank you," replied David, still wondering exactly what it was he was supposed to do with it. "I will."

"Now tell your folks, if they wants any proper vegetables - not them chemical-filled things they buys back home, come and see me."

And with that, she disappeared back inside her tiny house and closed the door. David examined his garlic closely from all angles, while Gary stood deep in thought, with a worried look on his face. He eventually spoke, addressing his friend in the same hushed, secretive fashion favoured by Guido Fawkes as he explained the gunpowder plot to his fellow Catholic conspirators in a shadowy London alehouse.

"David, listen. I *knew* I'd heard that word somewhere before, and now I remember where I heard it."

"What word?"

"Garlics."

"Oh, right!"

"Look, let's move away from the house, or she might hear us. You haven't got a telly, have you?"

"Not yet, but dad says…"

"I haven't got one either. Nor Mally, but Brett Spittle's mom and dad have."

"So what? They probably nicked it, mom says."

"Have you heard of Doctor Who?"

"Yes. You or Mally mentioned it up at the church the other day, and I heard a chap in the playground talking about it. He says there's a doctor, who isn't really a doctor, and he flies round the universe in a blue police box, fighting baddies and aliens and stuff. He said it was really scary as well!"

"That's right. I overheard Brett Spittle talking about it to Shaun Mulligan. He said that it wasn't made up, it was real."

David looked at his friend quizzically. "What do you mean, real? It's just a television programme isn't it?"

"Brett told Shaun that his dad said it was actually true – you know, like Robin Hood was true. The people on the telly are actors, he said, but there really is a Doctor who can travel around the universe, and that was what the programme was based on."

"I've never heard of that!" frowned David.

"That's because you haven't got a telly. There's a lot of news on the telly that we can't hear, because we haven't got tellies. The Americans are sending rockets into outer space all the time, so it *could* happen. Shaun said it wasn't true as well, but then Brett punched him on the nose hard and said it was, and he said he'd hit him again if Shaun said it wasn't."

"Oh, fair enough."

"But listen. This is what I'm trying to tell you, if you'd stop interrupting me. I heard Brett tell Shaun that Doctor Who has a really scary deadly enemy, and they're sort of like robots, but there's a little brain thing inside that works them, and they're called Garlics."

"Are you sure?"

"Positive. As soon as I saw that strange woman's sign, I knew I'd heard it before. Think about it, Dave. It all makes sense. She said that they were incredibly powerful didn't she? You wouldn't say a blooming vegetable was powerful, would you? You might say tasty, or sour, or sweet, or horrible if it was a Brussels sprout, but not powerful. And she said Garlics could kill bacteria. Well, there's lots of bacteria in outer space, because Mr Perriman said so."

"Yeah," said David excitedly, warming to the theme, "and she said that the doctor was her enemy too."

"And didn't she say that she was from another planet?"

"Definitely! I heard that, but I can't see how this little egg thing in my hand could attack Doctor Who, or turn into a flipping robot. Perhaps you got the word wrong."

"I *didn't*. Those things don't look much yet, but the weird woman said herself, she has to grow them. That's just a garlic egg, remember. I bet those pods hatch out and turn into robots. I bet she's got thousands of them in her back garden, and she's getting ready to take over the universe."

"Why would she want to do that?"

"It's what they all do, these baddies. It's the same in Dan Dare, only with him it's the Mekon. They take over universes. It's their hobby, I suppose."

David placed the garlic bulb in the grass.

"I'll leave it here then."

"You can't do that. Take it to school and show Mr Lewis. He'll know what to do with it."

David stood his ground. "Fair enough, but you can flipping carry it!"

CHAPTER 4

The Cricket Cup

Gary had promised to call for David at the house on Monday morning, and walk to school with him. Traditionally, Black Country children never knocked on the door but instead, literally 'called for' their friends, which, presumably, was where the expression came from. He shuffled up to the outhouse door and shouted "DAY-VED!" until David opened it and came bouncing out, closely followed by Ruby, who wished them a pleasant day. Gary, being a polite child, seized this opportunity to thank Mrs Day one last time for a lovely weekend, though she assured him that this was not necessary. He had, after all, already thanked her six times on Saturday and throughout Sunday, at every available opportunity.

After their adventure with the Strange Woman, they had returned to the caravan, only to be reprimanded by Ruby for ignoring her instructions about talking to strangers, and by the sound of it, this particular stranger was very strange indeed. Normally, Ruby would not have been so cautious, but the newspapers were full of stories about Yorkshire children being abducted. The police were sounding very concerned, and searching Saddleworth Moors, and many feared that the poor victims would not be found alive. Len, however, had urged her to calm down, assuring her that Tenbury was still a safe haven. When the children were safely out of earshot, he also reminded her that, sadly, it was usually men, not women, that children needed to be wary of.

The boys deliberately omitted to mention that the Strange Woman had given them a present, and the garlic bulb was hidden in a shoebox under David's bunk bed. In between the fishing expedition and the trip to the Regal Cinema, they nervously examined the box for signs of change, but none came. On Sunday teatime, as the Austin Cambridge pulled away from the site, Len was unaware that he had a sinister extra passenger stowed away on board - one that would not only wreak havoc but also change their lives forever.

* * *

Mr Perriman, headmaster of Brierley Bank Junior School, stood behind his impressive, carved oak lectern with the Staffordshire Knot motif, and addressed his flock.

"Good Morning, children. I hope you all had an enjoyable weekend, and you're refreshed and ready to use those brains of yours again. The older children will be sitting their eleven-plus exams this year, so I trust you are all going to bed early, getting lots of healthy exercise and eating lots of fish! Speaking of exercise, can I remind you all that the house cricket competition will begin next week, so Mr Lewis will soon be picking teams and running after-school training sessions. The Brierley Bank Junior School Cricket Cup is currently held by Red House, and they won it the previous year too, so come on Yellow, Green and Blue Houses, it's about time you took it off them. If you'd like to be

42

considered for your house team, see Mr Lewis after assembly and put your name down."

"You can count me out," whispered Gary. "I can't run, I can't bat, I can't bowl and I can't field. Looks like I'm the scorer again. Trouble is, I can't add up either!"

"I suppose I'll have to put my name down again," whispered David. "I can't do worse than last year, can I? I was out first ball, and then I bowled so badly that I hit Peter Fisher in the eye when he was fielding, and he had to go off."

"Was he standing too close to the batsman then?"

"No, that's just it. He was *behind* me at the time. I think I let go too early, or late, or something. I'm not cut out for sports. Why can't they have a cup for art?"

A stern look and a little cough from Mr Lewis, who was keeping an eye on things halfway down the hall, curtailed their conversation for the time being. Once assembly was concluded, David and Gary picked up where they had left off, en-route to their form room.

"Talking of sport, how's the Subbuteo going?" asked Gary. "Are you any good at it yet?"

"Average," confessed David, "They go the opposite way to where I try and flick them, but that might be my team's fault. They've got about sixteen broken legs between them, the goalie is a limbo dancer, and now I've gone and lost Mike Doyle's head. It was in the box – I know it was – and it's disappeared, so I'm going to look stupid when I play my first league match on Saturday. The good news is, dad's promised to get me a brand new Manchester City team for my birthday."

"What will you do with the busted team then?" asked Gary.

"Chuck them in the pedal bin probably."

"That's a shame!"

"Well, who'd want them in that state?"

"You did!"

"True. You can have them if you like."

"I don't know how to play and I haven't got a pitch," said Gary.

"Well, why don't you come round after school and I'll show you," offered David. "If you like it, you can keep my old Manchester City team, just to get you started, but you'd have to paint them another colour, because we can't have two people in the league using the same team. You can always share my pitch for the time being."

"That sounds good," smiled Gary. "It's the only kind of football I could manage to play, with my wonky leg. What teams are left to pick? I suppose all the good ones have been chosen now, if the league is starting soon."

"There's a list pinned up on our notice board in 6L," replied David, but all the first division sides have been picked now. Why don't you choose a second division team?"

"Like who?"

"I dunno. I only know the names of the first division." He suddenly began to convulse with laughter. "Why not choose Brierley Bank Celtic? My granddad used to play for them when he was young, but they're rubbish! That would be funny! Brierley Bank Celtic playing against the likes of Manchester United and Liverpool in the football league. They'd get hammered!"

"The same will happen in the Subbuteo league if I'm in charge of them," shrugged his friend. "What colour strip do they wear?"

"It's very nice actually. Green and white hoops, white shorts, green socks."

"Forget it! I could never paint hoops on a half-inch man's shirt - not with my eyesight."

"No, but I could!"

* * *

First lesson was Art with Mr Lewis. He pinned up the class's churchyard efforts and stood back to cast his less-than expert eye over them. With all the excitement of the weekend in Tenbury Wells, the falling tree incident had almost been forgotten about. It was Mally Lobes who was first to raise his hand.

"Sir, sir! Have you still got that letter, sir?"

"Oh yes, I meant to give it back to the vicar. Which reminds me – he said he'd try and find out a little more about our sad Mr Silversmith from the parish records. I'll pop to the church and see how he's doing. I must confess, I went to the library this weekend to find information about any Victorian carpenters that worked in Brierley Bank, but I couldn't find a sausage!"

"Sir, sir! I've asked my dad to look into it as well," called Gary from the back of the room. "He's in a local history society. I'll let you know if he comes up with something."

"Thank you, Gary. I'd appreciate that. Now let's turn our attention to your churchyard artwork. Right, David, excellent as always, well done! Malcolm, a nice picture, but would we necessarily expect to find a rainbow trout in a graveyard? Brett, I can't draw, as you all know, but if I'd dipped my pet spider in ink and let it walk all over the page, the results would have been better than your effort – and if I find out that it was you who cut the tops off those daffodils, you're for the slipper. Sarah, when I asked for a brass rubbing, I didn't mean the brass sign on the gentlemen's lavatories. George, which way up is it supposed to be then? Right, Henry, why have you drawn a picture of a German soldier covered in swastikas being machine-gunned senseless by an aeroplane? I know I was darting all over the churchyard, lad, but I think I would have heard if that was going on."

To a backdrop of stifled snorts and giggles, Mr Lewis ploughed gamely on, trying his best to give praise wherever possible, and temper criticism of his gentler and more delicate souls to avoid tears. He did feel some sympathy, after all, and secretly doubted he could have done any better. Had it not been against the school's policy, he would seriously have entertained the notion of allowing ten-year-old David Day to take the class for art, while he slipped off for a coffee and biscuits in the staff room. If the lad continued to progress at his present rate, he'd surely be repainting the Sistine Chapel ceiling by the time he was fourteen.

At first break, David, Gary and Mally sat on the low wall at the edge of the playground drinking their milk, which was, as usual, the wrong temperature. In summer it was almost cheese, and in winter it resembled a miniature vista of the North Pole in a bottle. David and Gary excitedly explained about the Strange Woman from Tenbury and her Garlic Egg. Once he had got over the initial slight of not being invited to the caravan himself, Mally Lobes was, quite literally, all ears.

Malcolm Stevens, to give him his real name, was an expert on all aspects of country life, such as bird-watching, egg collecting and fishing. He was also a keen amateur taxidermist, and his bedroom was always full of dead creatures awaiting surgery, much to his mother's distress. Often, on returning home from a hard day at the galvanized bucket factory, she would head for the fridge to make a snack, only to find a deceased squirrel next to the cheese, or a road-kill barn owl nestled on top of her egg box. The art of taxidermy takes years of practice, and young Malcolm had, in fairness, only been an enthusiast for just over a year and a half, which meant that most of his creations appeared a little lop-sided, and some had peculiar fixed grins or cross-eyed grimaces. The squirrel on a lump of bark that he had given David for his tenth birthday had been relegated to the loft by Ruby, who accused it of sneering at her.

Physically, Malcolm closely resembled the Brierley Bank Junior School Cricket Cup, in that he possessed a pair of ears that a pipistrelle bat would have died for, hence his nickname, Mally Lobes, Physically, he was no oil painting, unless one included the works of Arthur Rackham, but when advice was called for on mysterious flora and fauna, Mally was your man. David had expressed a feeling of nervousness about keeping his Garlic egg under his bed at home, in case the robots hatched unexpectedly, but Mally, who was made of sterner stuff, had no such qualms. A boy who had a bedroom that resembled an animal mortuary could deal with a mere egg full of baby robots.

David, heartened by this news, felt the weight of the world roll off his back. For all he knew, the whole thing was probably a load of nonsense, but one couldn't be too sure. He wasn't a superstitious child, but he reckoned that it paid to not walk under ladders, just in case. The same applied to harbouring Garlic eggs under beds. It was his birthday the following day – a day he was dreading due to a ritual known as The Bumps – but thanks to his parent's generosity, there was also something to look forward to. During the dinnertime break, he was going to make the short journey up the High Street to Miss Kettle's Toy and Joke Shop to purchase his Manchester City Subbuteo team, and he couldn't wait. He also promised to wrap the garlic egg in tissue paper and bring it to school in his pocket, so that Mally could take over custody and examine it at leisure. The more David thought about this silly egg, the more he realized it was nothing more than a made-up story. Gary had probably heard the word wrong, and it wasn't 'garlic' at all. He couldn't imagine how robots could grow from pods inside a little white egg. It made no sense whatsoever. On the other hand, the Strange Woman *had* said she was from another planet, and she had made a point of warning them how powerful the egg was. She'd also told them that she was a sworn enemy of the doctor. The egg didn't seem as if it was about to burst open, that was for sure, but it was silly to take chances. Mally had offered to keep it safe, so he was welcome to it.

CHAPTER 5

A Visit from the Doctor

It was Tuesday, the twenty-seventh of April, and a very excited David Day was eating cornflakes at the breakfast table. His beloved dad sat opposite, wolfing down his beans on toast before dashing to work. Len was thirty-five years old with dark, greased back hair that barely concealed a small bald patch beneath. He was well-built, thanks to years of having to manhandle heavy pieces of steel, in sharp contrast to his dreamy son, who was built along the lines of a toothpick, thanks to a couple of years spent handling very small paintbrushes.

"Happy Birthday, son!" he beamed, handing him a small envelope inscribed with exactly the same sentiment. "Eleven today! Have I ever told you, you were due to be born on the nineteenth, according to the midwife, but you were late arriving? That would have been one day after Spike Milligan's birthday – that's probably where you get your sense of humour from."

"And one day before Hitler, according to mom," moaned David, "and that's probably where I get my hairstyle from."

49

"Well, have a nice time, and if I were you, I'd hide at playtime, so as you don't get the bumps."

David winced at the thought. He hated having a birthday or a haircut on school days. If it wasn't the bumps, it was getting whacked around the back of the head, with some idiot screaming 'haircut!' in his ear.

Len rubbed his son's shoulders and donned his donkey jacket, ready for work. David said goodbye, thanked his parents for the money and dashed upstairs to his bedroom. He gingerly retrieved the garlic egg from beneath his bed, blew the dust off it and wrapped it in toilet paper before slipping it into his trouser pocket, alongside his birthday envelope. He collected his blazer and satchel, kissed his mother farewell and set off on the short walk to school. David was itching to try out his new Subbuteo team, and to this end, had asked Gary to come round that evening. He could show his friend how to play, and if there was time afterwards, repair and re-paint his old team so that Gary could take them away and practise. The league was to begin the following evening, and David had been drawn to play away at Ian Garrington's house, a few streets away. Garrington was a small, chubby individual who had bagged West Ham United. He was a very bossy child who, whilst never yet resorting to actual physical violence, was verbally intimidating and had a short temper. Even worse than that, he was reputedly one of the best Subbuteo players in the school, so David was dreading the encounter. Garrington would almost certainly have his gang of mates around for the first ever game, and David knew full well what a difference a big home crowd could make.

50

First playtime came all too soon, and David stepped nervously into the playground, trying to look inconspicuous. He'd toyed with the idea of spending his birthday money on a false beard from Miss Kettle's shop, but decided against it, as hirsute eleven-year-olds tended to stand out like sore thumbs, which somewhat defeated the object.

It was only a matter of seconds until the baying hyenas had picked up his scent. Brett, Shaun and Ian Garrington were marching over to him, with malice aforethought.

"Grab him!" shouted Brett, roughly manhandling the quivering nervous wreck to the floor. Trevor Jones, the lad who had fleeced David with his injury-stricken Manchester City side, was quickly drafted in to grab the remaining limb.

David was then flung into the air so high that his weedy body was thrown inside out, like a parachute, and then roughly returned to earth, making sure that his bottom connected with the hard playground. This torture was repeated another ten times, each bump more aggressive than the last, until the count of eleven was completed.

"One for luck," screamed Brett Spittle, flinging David even higher than before. "Now let go!"

David was left floating in space, unsupported by his antagonists. He fell to earth heavily on his back, cracking his head on the playground, and began to cry. He desperately didn't want to shed tears, but he couldn't help it. Mally ran over to help his stricken friend, once he had seen what was going on, and Gary came shuffling awkwardly behind him.

"That was for telling on me to your mother!" snarled Brett, as he walked away. "The next time, it'll be worse than that."

51

"That was too rough, Brett!" interjected Mally. "You could have broken his back."

"And I'll break your nose next, if you say one more word!" spat Brett, his face contorted with hatred.

Mally decided that, on this occasion, discretion was the better part of valour, and turned away in disgust. Mr Lewis, who had been on playground duty at the other end of the school, heard the commotion and ran over to investigate. He helped David to his feet and asked what had happened. Once his huge, shuddering sobs had subsided, he was able to reply, but perhaps due to the trauma, seemed unable to remember the names of the guilty. Thankfully, he had survived his ordeal with only minor injuries, but this was more by luck than judgment.

After a morning that seemed to go on forever, dinnertime finally arrived, and David skipped up the High Street, trying his best to put the unpleasant memories of first playtime behind him. His mother had commented only that morning that birthdays became less pleasant when one was older. He could have told her that they weren't a bundle of laughs when one was young either. Now he had one more ordeal to endure before the new Subbuteo team was truly his. It was time to do battle with the dreaded Miss Kettle, a woman that even Trolls were frightened of.

He took a deep breath and entered the shop to the sound of a tinkling bell. Miss Kettle glided out from her private quarters, as if on castors. She was so small that David could glimpse no more than her head and shoulders above the counter, but that was more than enough to put the fear of God into him. Physically, she looked very similar to Ena Sharples, of Coronation Street fame, or the grandmother from the famous Giles cartoons. Character-wise – as if *they* weren't bad enough - she was more akin to the Wicked Witch of the West.

"Yes?" she barked. She believed in brevity being the soul of wit.

"Erm, can I have a Manchester City Subbuteo team please?" asked David, quaking.

"I'll have to get the steps," growled Miss Kettle, annoyed. She fetched a small set of steps from her private quarters and positioned them so that she could just about reach the stack of white boxes on her blackened, heavily-varnished shelf.

"Manchester, you say?"

"Yes please."

She pulled out a box, examined the sticker on the end panel and clambered down the steps.

"That's ten bob," she snarled.

David nervously dug into his trouser pockets and produced his tissue-wrapped garlic bulb.

"Er, s-sorry, wrong pocket," he stammered, placing it on the counter. He rummaged some more and produced a dog-eared envelope this time, which he duly handed over. Miss Kettle snatched it, opened it and examined the contents at close quarters through the half-inch thick lenses of her spectacles.

"That's right," she grunted. "Here you are."

David took the box, which she'd wrapped in a plain white bag, and thanked her profusely. It is strange how the English make such an effort to be nicer than usual to people who are downright rude. Miss Kettle dropped the cash into her ornate brass till, responded with another grunt and glided back whence she came. David skipped out of the shop and, realizing that time was marching on, ran back down the High Street to catch the last few minutes of playtime.

Five minutes later, the doorbell of Miss Kettle's Toy and Joke Shop rang once more, and in walked a rather dapper looking man wearing a pinstriped suit and trilby. He was sporting a pencil-thin black moustache, which, for some reason best known to himself, sat not on his top lip but fully a half inch above it. He was carrying a large, black case in his left hand and a business card in his right.

Miss Kettle came charging out once more, irritated at the sound of her own doorbell. Her mood was not sweetened much by the presence of Chas Higgins either. It was bad enough having to serve people who threw money at her, but it was almost unbearable when those who entered her lair only did so with the intention of picking her pocket.

"What do *you* want?" she growled.

"Ah, Miss Kettle, good day to you," began Chas, doffing his trilby. "How are the stocks? Need anything this week, do we?"

"We don't."

"How about whoopee cushions? Chocolate cigarettes maybe? Plastic dog turds? I see you're down to your last three."

"No thank you."

"Never mind eh? That's not really what I came for. I've got something brand new in my case that's going to make you a fortune. Hot off the press, these are, and I personally guarantee that they'll be best sellers. If not, I promise to eat my hat. Now, can I put you down for a dozen? These things will fly out of the shop, or I'm a Dutchman."

"What's this?" asked Miss Kettle, unimpressed.

"What's what?" asked Chas.

"This little parcel," replied Miss Kettle, prodding the package on her counter.

"Nothing to do with me," Chas assured her.

* * *

"So where is it then?" asked Mally eagerly, as the three friends stood in the playground at afternoon break.

"Here!" David replied, "In my pocket. I've kept it well hidden in case Mr Perriman confisticated it." He delved deep, his facial expression changing to one of anguish. "At least it was there. It's gone."

"What do you mean, it's gone?"

"It was definitely there this morning, and I know it was there at playtime, because I kept feeling it to see if it was about to burst open," explained David nervously.

"The bumps!" groaned Gary. "I bet is came out of your trousers when they gave you the bumps."

David trawled through his memory banks. Did he remember feeling it after playtime? He couldn't be sure.

"Did you go anywhere lunchtime with it? Have you taken it back home and left it there?"

"No, I didn't go home. I went to – hang on, that's it! I've left it at Miss Kettle's shop. I was looking for my money and I put it on the counter."

"Genius!" sighed Gary. "Did you actually remember to pick up your Subbuteo team? You're such a daydreamer, David!"

"Oh yes, I remembered that. Here it is."

David reached inside his satchel and pulled out the white box. Checking to see that Brett and his gang were safely over the far side of the playground, he lifted the lid. He'd have done so before, but he had arrived back at school just as the bell rang, and double maths had prevented him from examining his purchase. As the lid was removed, his facial expression changed once more from expectation to desperation, just as the boy in the Fry's Five Boys Chocolate advertisement did, but the other way round.

"Flippineck!" he groaned, tousling up his Hitler hairdo in frustration. "I don't believe it! She's only gone and given me Manchester United! I'm going to have to dash back up to her shop at four o'clock and change it. That means I have to deal with Miss flipping Kettle twice in one day."

"Well, at least you can get the garlic egg back while you're there," said Mally. "I really wanted to study that tonight."

"Okay!" replied David, "here's the plan. Gary, you've told your mom you're coming back for tea at my house, right? Me and Mally will go to Kettle's right after school, and you get back to my house and tell mother I won't be long, or else she'll worry about me being abdicated by aliens or Yorkshire people. Miss Kettle's is on the way home for Mally, so he can study his egg tonight."

The three friends agreed the plan, and returned to their classroom for science.

At five minutes to four, chairs were placed on tables and noisy pupils were told to face the front till the bell went. Five minutes later, three hundred screaming children streamed out of Brierley Bank Junior School, heading home for their Heinz Tomato soup, their fish fingers and their bread and butter. David and Mally ran as fast as their legs could carry them, straight into Miss Kettle's shop.

The shop's eponymous owner glided out from her sitting room and glared at the two breathless boys.

"What?" she asked.

"Sorry, Miss Kettle," David gasped, "only I asked for Manchester City, and you gave me Manchester United."

Miss Kettle sighed so heavily that Mally thought she would deflate. She grabbed her steps and wearily hobbled over to the Subbuteo shelf, snatching David's team box as she did so. She replaced the box and scanned the shelf for its replacement. After perusing the labels from no more than two inches away, she eventually selected a box and climbed down her steps, thrusting it into David's hands. If David had asked her to remove her own heart using a rusty penknife without anaesthetic, she couldn't have looked more put out. David decided that it would be a good idea to check for himself this time. He lifted the lid and smiled. Sky blue with claret bands on the socks. Perfect! He thanked her and walked out of the shop, closely followed by an exasperated looking Mally.

"Have you forgotten something?" he asked David as they stood next to the shop window. "What about my garlic egg?"

David wasn't listening, however. He was staring at the shop window with his mouth wide open. At the front of the window display, next to the plastic dog turd, were twelve small but perfectly formed Daleks.

"Oh my God!" cried David, reeling. He suddenly felt the need to cling onto the window ledge as a means of support. "They've hatched!"

Now it was Mally's turn not to listen. He was far too busy staring at the pavement opposite Miss Kettle's shop. The object of his fascination was something he'd never seen before, and it definitely hadn't been there when he'd walked home on Monday evening. He silently clutched at David's blazer and gestured for him to turn round. As David did so, his blood ran cold, and the hairs on the back of his neck stood to attention.

He was looking at a large blue police box.

CHAPTER 6

Granddad's head is missing!

David had plenty to tell Gary about when he burst into the house, some ten minutes after his terrifying experiences in the High Street. He dragged him up to the privacy of his cramped little bedroom and filled him in, omitting no detail, however slight. Gary received the news as would a halibut, or for that matter, any species of fish. He just stared at David goggle-eyed, his mouth wide open, as if gasping for air in a landing net.

"I've got to see this for myself!" he eventually croaked.

"It's too late now," replied David, "and besides, we have to sort out the Subbuteo teams. We'll go to the shop in our dinnertime break tomorrow."

Gary agreed that this was a good idea.

"Are you absolutely sure you and Mally weren't halluminating?" Gary continued. "Miss Kettle can have that effect on people, you know."

David assured him that both of them had seen the garlic robots and the police box with their own eyes. Mally had even crossed the road and tapped on it, before running back terrified. It was definitely real.

"Look, it's no good getting worked up about it tonight," said Gary. "Let's just go back downstairs and take our mind off things with a game of Subbuteo."

After consuming the mandatory fish fingers, David laid out his pitch and proudly showed Gary his new team. He then produced the old Manchester City team, by way of contrast.

"Wow!" said Gary, deeply unimpressed. "Wonky Legs United. The perfect team for me!"

David had to agree that they wouldn't fetch much in the way of transfer fees in their current state. However, Len had promised to glue them properly when he got home from work, as he didn't want Gary to inherit a team of footballers in such a poor state of health - his pride wouldn't allow it. Len was a perfectionist – a state of mind that wasn't so much something to be proud of, but more akin to an illness. David too was a perfectionist, but there are two distinct types. Those who meticulously plan their projects and execute them with military precision, and those who rush into things, make a complete pig's ear of them, and then stroppily insist on starting all over again, cursing and spitting as they do so. David, unlike his father, fell into the latter category. He eyed his ex-team with self-loathing and disgust, ashamed that he could have been so slapdash and shoddy, especially as his friend was to be the recipient of this team of no-hopers.

"Okay, I admit they don't look in perfect condition at the moment," he admitted, "but when dad's finished with them, and I've painted them up, they'll be like new. Till then, why don't I show you how to play?"

David quickly explained the rudiments of the game and allowed Gary a few practise flicks. He explained how it was possible to make the players spin and weave around their opponents by flicking the sides of the bases, as one would apply side to a snooker ball. He also emphasized the importance of not losing possession, and demonstrated how to make the ball rise in the air when a shot at goal was taken, to make it harder for the goalie to deal with. Gary watched closely, taking it all in, and even pausing occasionally to make notes on a scrap of paper with David's thirteen colour biro.

"Okay, enough theory," insisted David. "Let's have a game."

If Gary was hampered by the assortment of gammy legs on display, he didn't let it show, and never once complained when one of his players suddenly lurched off at some unexpected angle, or simply fell in half. Perhaps he felt an affinity for his less-than athletic side, and thought it hypocritical to criticize their erratic performance. After having lived with similar problems all of his life, he certainly didn't feel the need to offer excuses. He just pressed on gamely, seemingly enjoying every minute.

The first match saw Manchester City beat Brierley Bank Celtic four-one, but, all things considered, this wasn't too bad. For one, Gary had never played before, and state of his handicapped side was hardly conducive to fluid match-play. He'd also had a couple of near misses, when his headless striker glanced the crossbar, so it could easily have been four-three, he argued. And then there was the dubious penalty decision that was denied him. If all else failed, Gary could have made a successful career for himself as a football pundit, such was the quality of his post-match analysis.

Len arrived from work, tired and dirty, and proceeded to wash himself at the kitchen sink, stripped down to his white vest. After half an hour with the Express and Star, followed by smoked haddock and chips, he volunteered to begin rebuilding Gary's sorry team. Firstly, he scraped off copious amounts of surplus glue with a craft knife, tut-tutting at his embarrassed son as he did so. Then he repaired to his tool shed, where each stricken player was lightly clamped in a model-maker's vice and examined through a huge angle-poise magnifying glass. Minute amounts of a powerful, quick setting plastic glue were neatly applied to severed knees, ankles and arms, and limbs were expertly tweezered back into place. Then, when they were thoroughly dry, they were handed over to David at the kitchen table to transform them into Brierley Bank Celtic while a hushed and reverent Gary looked on.

"They look brand new now," he grinned, thrilled to bits. "Thank you, Mr Day. Thank you David!"

"Now all we need is a team sheet," mumbled David, his tongue poking out at jaunty angles with sheer concentration.

"A what?"

"A team sheet. A list of your players' names."

"I can supply that," smiled Ruby, jumping up from her armchair and dashing to the teak cabinet in the living room. Seconds later, she was back with an old black and white photograph.

"This is Brierley Bank Celtic in nineteen-forty-six, just after the war. There's your granddad Reuben, second from the right, front row."

"Wow!" said David. "I've never seen this before. Look at those shorts! And the tops, with those huge collars. All the players look about fifty as well."

"Well they weren't," Ruby assured him. "People just seemed to look older in those days, for some reason. Look, the names are on the back."

She showed David and Gary the faded brown writing, and David remarked on how neat it was, compared to writing in the sixties. The list read:

Back Row.

Jack Bannock (Captain), Arthur Foley, George Foley, Richard Green (Goalkeeper), Barry Edwards, Maurice Billingham.

Front Row.

Leonard Garrington, Reuben Cole, Harold Carpenter, Percy Shakespeare, Herbert Groves (Reserve) Wilf Priest, Bert James (Trainer).

"Right, well that's my names sorted out then," grinned Gary.

"All we have to do now," added Len, "is to find granddad Reuben's head. David's gone and lost it somehow. He swears it was loose in his box, but I can't find it."

Ruby seemed affronted by this remark. "How come it has to be my dad's head that's missing? I thought it was Mike Summerbee's head that was missing."

"No," corrected David. "It was Mike Doyle's head that was missing, actually, but Mike Doyle is now granddad Reuben."

Ruby, sensing that one of David's unfathomable episodes was coming on, disappeared to make a pot of tea.

"Somebody had scraped Mike Doyle's hair off, that's why, and it made him look like granddad, because he's bald," David called after her. Ruby had the expression of one who was none the wiser. He continued to apply the tiny green hoops with his 'oo' sable brush, until, at seven-thirty, he finally replaced the lids on his Humbrol Enamels and called it a day.

A knock on the outhouse door announced that Mr Leyton had arrived to collect his son for bathing purposes, it being a Wednesday. Gary wished the Days goodnight, and thanked them for having him, feeding him, mending and repainting his Subbuteo team, and anything else he could think of.

"Oh, before we go," interrupted Gary's father, Cyril, "I've been doing a bit of digging on our Mr Jeremiah Silversmith. No doubt David's told you the story. Well, I've trawled all the records I can find, and I even asked my fellow history society members to delve into whatever they'd got, especially about Brierley Bank, and we've come up with a big, fat, nothing. According to the parish records, Jeremiah Silversmith simply did not exist."

* * *

Thursday dinnertime saw David, Mally and Gary making their way up the steep High Street, so that Gary could see with his own eyes what had traumatized his two friends the day before. As they approached Miss Kettle's, they knew straightaway that something was amiss. Heads were scratched, and two thirds of those present were looking more than a little sheepish.

"I don't understand it!" moaned Mally. "It was definitely here yesterday, Gary. I touched it."

Mally was distraught. He had acted as Doubting Thomas to the police box's Jesus. He had crossed the busy main road and touched the thing, to confirm that it was not an apparition, and it was undisputedly flesh and blood. Well, wood and glass anyway. Now it had disappeared, and left not a wrack behind. Gary, meanwhile, had turned his attentions to Miss Kettle's shop window. He faced his co-conspirators with a stern look.

"And where, would you imagine, have the garlic robots gone, my hallucinating friends?"

Miss Kettle's display boasted a fine collection of peppery chewing gum, plastic dog turds, phony cigarettes and wind-up chattering teeth. What it was short of, however, was Daleks. There wasn't a solitary one to be had, for neither love nor money.

"This is crazy!" whined David, exasperated. "We both saw them, didn't we Mal?"

Mally said nothing. He just sat in the gutter, head in hands. After fully five minutes of awkward silence, during which Gary stared at a drainpipe and David kicked at dog-ends, they returned, crestfallen, to the delights of double maths.

That evening David crawled home, his mind in turmoil. They had definitely seen the police box, and now it was gone. Surely this meant that Doctor Who was not just some scary television programme, but real, as Brett had suggested. It pained David to agree with anything that Master Spittle said, but the evidence was there for all to see. Or rather, it had been, and now it wasn't again. It was obvious to the meanest intelligence - Brett in other words - that the Doctor had visited Brierley Bank in his time machine in search of garlics, and having found some lurking in Miss Kettle's shop, destroyed them with his ray-gun and time-travelled to some other trouble spot to do it all over again. This wasn't a case of trying to convince Gary that Doctor Who actually existed by showing him the evidence. It was the very *lack* of evidence that proved the theory, on this occasion. There was currently no Tardis in Brierley Bank High Street, therefore, Doctor Who exists. Case proven!

David would have given the whole conundrum a lot more thought, had it not been for his imminent league fixture. After reluctantly shovelling down one of Ruby's more bizarre attempts at a salad, he grabbed his new team, his duffel coat and balaclava, fastened his snake belt and headed for Woodland Avenue, the home of West Ham United F.C. Ian Garrington answered the door and let him into the front room, where a pitch mounted onto hardboard, brushed to perfection and boasting real, battery-powered floodlights awaited. Crammed onto the settee were Trevor Jones, Barry Raybould and Peter Fletcher, the gang he hung around with after school. Their role was to provide moral support for Ian, and intimidation for his opponent.

"Right, welcome to the first match of the nineteen-sixty-five Subbuteo league season," he announced grandly.

"Fifteen minutes per side, referee's decision is final – that's you Trev – three points to the winner, none to the loser, and a point each for a draw. Agreed?"

David nodded nervously.

"West Ham United versus Manchester City."

David opened his box and began to arrange his players on the pitch.

"Where's the team I swapped you?" asked Trevor. "They'm new 'uns!"

"I gave them to Gary Leyton. He's thinking of entering the league."

"Too late!" insisted Ian Garrington. "He didn't apply before the deadline. Besides, he's a spaz. He'd be hopeless."

"That's not very nice," frowned David. It wasn't the wisest move to criticize Ian Garrington before the game had even begun, but the words just seemed to fall out of his mouth.

The moment was diffused, thankfully, by the arrival of Ian's mother, who asked if the capacity crowd required biscuits and squash.

"Can Gary play in the F.A. Cup Final instead then?" asked David, with perfect and deliberate timing.

"Er, yeah, I suppose so," growled Ian, eager not to sound spiteful in front of his mother. He gave David a look that was intended to black his eye. Mrs Garrington disappeared whence she came with the food and beverages order.

"Anyway, what's his team going to be? We can't have two Manchester Cities."

"Brierley Bank Celtic," announced David. This was greeted with gales of laughter from the home supporters.

"That's about right," sneered Ian. "A spazzy team for a spazzy chap. Trev, blow the whistle."

Trevor did as he was told and the match was under way. Ian Garrington was indeed a skilful player. Within seconds, he'd juggled the ball into David's half, and scored a spectacular goal. The crowd went wild, and the whistle was blown. Back at the centre circle, David had managed to string a couple of passes together and was advancing on Garrington's goal, when suddenly the chubby little fellow called out "Blocks!"

"What's that?" queried David. He had been careful to familiarize himself with every line of the rule book, and nowhere had he seen that word used. He gave the referee a quizzical look, and the referee did likewise to Ian Garrington.

"If the other chap's team is advancing on my goal, but he's only got, one, two, three players in my half, I can call 'blocks' and he's got to give me time to rearrange my players in front of the goals to block his shot."

"I've never heard of that," admitted Trevor. Garrington gave him one of his searing looks.

"Oh yes, I remember, the, erm, blocks rule. Okay, carry on!"

Garrington arranged his men so that the goal mouth was completely protected. David shook his head, but was asked to hurry up and stop time-wasting, or he'd be penalized. He took a shot, which bounced harmlessly off Garrington's battalion of players. Seconds later, the ball was in the back of David's net once more. It was two-nil to West Ham.

Garrington attacked once again, and his players were now dangerously close to David's goal. David reached for his keeper in anticipation of a shot.

"Pelunty!" declared Garrington, raising his arms in celebration.

"Why?" asked David, frustrated. "What did I do?"

"You moved your keeper before I took my shot," snarled Garrington. That's a pelunty!"

"That's only when you're actually *taking* a penalty, surely?" insisted David. "Not when it's just a shot in a normal game."

"Pelunty!" declared Trevor.

"That's not fair!" moaned David.

" 'Tis!" argued Garrington. "So shurrup!"

By halftime, David was six-nil down, and worse was to come in the second half. Garrington, in attempting to reach over the pitch to flick a player, knelt on the new Mike Summerbee, snapping his legs in two. From then on, David seemed to lose the will to live, and conceded another fourteen goals. He pulled on his duffel coat and balaclava, reluctantly shook hands and trudged home, his first league match lost by a considerable margin. He was sure that Garrington had cheated, which was galling, as he was skilful enough to have won fairly. David amused himself by repeating all the words that he had heard the brutish little horror mispronounce during the match, mantra-like.

"Pelunty – Sumbarine – Semi-Cirtle - Miggle – Sustificate – Pelunty – Sumbarine – Miggle - Sustificate..."

He didn't know why, but it just made him feel a bit better.

CHAPTER 6

A stitch in time saves three

It was Saturday morning, and David was on the residents' car park at the back of his house with Mally, practising his batting. Every time he'd played in the cricket competition, he'd been out more or less first ball, and he needed to improve somewhat. Mally bowled him a nice, slow delivery, just to give him half a chance, having asked David to try and go for blocks, rather than attempting to hit everything for a six. The lad had a tendency to try and go for glory with every ball, and it had often proved his undoing. Whether it was unexpectedly hearing the word 'blocks' again that had fired him up, or merely the fact that he possessed a three-second attention span, is not known. His reaction to Mally's slow ball was uncharacteristically assertive, and bordering on the Don Bradman. David launched the tennis ball over the corrugated asbestos garage roofs and back into his own garden, much to Mally's surprise and delight.

"We'll make a cricketer of you yet!" he called, clapping in appreciation.

David rocketed off across the car park and disappeared down the narrow gap between his dad's and the neighbour's garage to retrieve the ball. A second later, an ear-piercing shriek cut through the air like a knife. Running over to see what on earth had happened, Mally found David grasping his leg and looking slightly whiter than a bottle of school milk. Mally edged his way sideways down the channel, which was only around a foot and a half wide, until he was next to his stricken friend.

"What on earth have you done?" he asked, worried by David's ghostly countenance.

David hobbled through the narrow space into his garden and fell to the ground, sobbing uncontrollably. He nervously removed his grubby hand, expecting the worst, and was not disappointed. There was a four inch by half an inch gash in the side of his knee, with a piece of flesh approximately the size of a big fat chip completely missing. Mally thought he could see part of David's bone showing, but couldn't be sure. It was certainly white, and curiously, there was hardly any blood at all.

David, who wasn't the bravest of children, took one look and passed out on the lawn. Ruby heard the shriek from the kitchen, where she was preparing a beef stew for when Len got home, and came dashing out, still wiping her hands on her pinafore. She saw her darling child spark-out, with a demented-looking Mally Lobes dancing around beside him. As she ran to take a closer look, Len pulled into his garage, with the Austin Cambridge belting out smoke from its engine compartment. He staggered through the garage door, his hand wrapped in what looked like fifty yards of red and white bandage.

"I've blinking gashed myself with a blinking chisel!" he winced. Here was a man who had never been known to

72

swear, even when he had gashed his blinking hand with a chisel.

Len Day was used to cuts and bruises. As a toolmaker of some fifteen years standing, it was expected that occasionally he would cop the odd injury, and he had grown accustomed to it. If limbs were hacked off, he would merely apply a band-aid and continue to earn his daily bread. He had no particular fear of blood, though obviously, he preferred not to lose too much of it. Ruby, on the other hand, was squeamish in the extreme. She had to ask her husband to accompany David to his many surgery injections, as even a fleeting glimpse of the needle could render her unconscious. She reached the disaster area all of a flutter and was confronted by not one, but two of her nearest and dearest sporting particularly awful injuries. True to form, she duly fainted.

Len, upon seeing his wife in a heap and his only son likewise with a fairly sizable piece of his leg completely missing, began to flap, just as Mally was doing. He seemed to be just running around like a headless chicken, undecided on whom he should tend to first, a decision made all the more difficult by the fact that he was bleeding profusely himself. Then, just when he thought things couldn't get any worse, they did. Either the next door neighbour was killing at least six pigs simultaneously with a penknife, or Clive Homer, Mrs Homer's fourteen-year-old, had done himself some serious damage. Thankfully, the latter was the case. Mrs Homer popped her head over the fence and begged Len to come to her aid. Clive had been standing with his hand resting against the outhouse back-door frame chatting to his mother, when a sudden gust of wind blew through the open front door, dramatically slamming the door shut where her son stood. After his pig-like squealing had died down, he had noticed, at exactly the same time as an excruciating pain seared through his body, that his little finger, a personal favourite, was staring up at him from the grass.

This latest revelation plunged Len into deep and unfathomable waters. He began ruffling his hair distractedly and emitting a strange whining noise.

"I'll get the car!" he eventually blurted. "Mally, try and wake Ruby up, I need help – erm, or David. No, leave him be, while he's unconscious, he's not in any pain. Mrs Homer, can you find Clive's finger? Put it in cotton wool and find a matchbox. Bandage his finger. No, sorry, bandage where his finger *used* to be, and don't faint on me, or we're all knackered."

He dashed to the car and placed his keys in the ignition. The Austin Cambridge just made a frustrating 'her-her-her-her' sound and refused to start. The car appeared to be mocking him now - taunting him and laughing like a jackass. Thinking on his feet, Len commandeered the large old coach-built pram which Ruby had stored in the garage when David outgrew it. He dashed back to the garden and gathered up his son, who was beginning to come round, and was sobbing with shock.

"Mal, how strong are you?" asked Len in desperation.

"Erm, er, quite, for my age," replied Mally nervously.

"Could you manage David on your back all the way up to Doctor Rodgerson's?"

"I'll try!"

74

"Good man! I'll place him on for you. Give him a donkey!"

Mrs Homer had appeared at the garage door with a white and shell-shocked Clive sporting a bandage almost identical to Len's own. Len helped lift him into the old pram and called Mally.

"Is Ruby waking up yet?"

"Yes."

"Good, let's go. I'll have to explain all this to her when I get back."

The cavalcade of invalids staggered out of the car park, sweating and grunting their way out of the housing estate and up the torturous High Street. After a few hundred yards, Mally was becoming cross-eyed with the strain of carrying his friend, and the journey was made all the worse by David's constant whimpering. Len, dripping blood down his work trousers, pushed the ghostly and unnervingly silent Clive until beads of sweat plopped from the end of his nose, with the severed finger safely stowed in the pocket of his donkey jacket. Bringing up the rear, Mrs Homer, still in carpet slippers, fretted, wailed and wrung her hands in anguish. Meanwhile, Ruby sat with her head between her legs on the grass, breathing heavily and wondering where everyone had gone.

After what seemed like an age, the exhausted walking wounded arrived at the front door of Doctor Rodgerson's surgery, and Len banged it in desperation. Within seconds, the door creaked open to reveal a middle-aged man with white, wild hair and a scarf around his neck. If this was

Doctor Katherine Rodgerson, thought Len, her looks had improved.

There were two general practitioners operating in Brierley Bank, at opposite ends of the High Street. Doctor Rodgerson was built along the lines of a female James Robertson Justice, star of the Doctor movies, with the accompanying gruff manner. Strangely, however, she was as gentle as a lamb when it came to administering injections. Doctor Fairbrother, on the other hand, was infinitely more feminine and gentle-natured, but had obviously trained as a vet at a Rhino sanctuary in Africa, if her needle technique was anything to go by. All this was purely by the by, as it happened, because the man who opened the surgery door fitted neither description.

"What on earth is the matter?" he asked, not unreasonably, on studying the motley crew before him. "Have you been in a road accident?"

Len quickly told the doctor what had befallen them, and they were dashed into the surgery. The doctor explained that he was a locum, merely standing in for Doctor Rodgerson for a couple of weeks, because she had gone to Brighton on holiday. He calmly assessed the situation and decided that Clive needed hospital treatment straight away. Packing the grisly severed finger in ice, he phoned for an ambulance and gave the boy strong painkillers. Next he asked to see Len's cut, which was quite deep, but Len explained that his son should come first. The doctor examined the boy's wound, and asked where the missing chunk of flesh had gone.

"Probably still hanging on that nail in Mr Day's garage," guessed Mally, to which David responded by fainting again.

"He'll need stitches, I'm afraid," frowned the good doctor, and began to prepare his equipment.

Mally made himself useful by opening the surgery door for the ambulance men. Shortly afterwards, Clive, his mother and the wayward digit left at speed for Corbett's Hospital.

The doctor duly brought David back to the land of the living with a sniff of smelling salts, and told him that he'd have to be brave, as what he was about to do would sting a little. This was in fact untrue. It stung a lot, but having Mally there with him helped. David would have to be stoic in front of a school friend. Had it just been his dad with him, he'd have cried his eyes out.

Ten excruciating stitches later, the job was done. A bandage was applied, painkillers administered, and for the first time in an hour or so, David felt up to giving everyone a weak, pitiful little smile. Next up was Len, but he insisted that the boys leave the room, as he didn't really want his son fainting for the third time. To this end, they were allowed to sit in the waiting room, where there was much to catch up with.

"Well, that's me out of the school cricket cup then," sighed David disconsolately. "Just when I was starting to get the flipping hang of it as well."

Mally wasn't listening, however. His attention was focused on developments outside in the street.

"Er, Dave," he said incredulously. "You are not going to believe this. Look out of the window."

David spun around in his chair, and what he saw caused him to gulp audibly. Right next to the side entrance to the surgery was the blue police box.

* * *

"You can come back in now," smiled the doctor. "Your father's been very brave."

David limped in, followed by a shaken Mally. The doctor was just about to continue, when he was interrupted by a loud banging at the front door. He sighed, made his excuses and left the room. Seconds later, he re-entered with Ruby Day in tow. She was looking flustered.

"Your wife, I believe!" smiled the doctor, sitting down behind his desk.

"I thought you'd all be here," she said. "What on earth has been going on?"

"Well, Mrs Day," said the doctor, "It appears that your husband was under the impression that it was cheaper for me to treat his entire family and near neighbours at the same time – a job lot! I can't tell you how much fun that was for me. Quite the best cure for constipation I have come across, in fact. Mr Day here has gashed his hand with a very sharp chisel at work, but he's stitched now and fine. Young master Homer is a concern, however. His finger..."

"You needn't tell Ruby all about...." interrupted Len.

"...was completely severed, so he's been dashed to hospital. Hopefully...."

"Only she sometimes..."

"And David here decided it would be a good idea to leave a sizable chunk of flesh hanging on a nail…"

"…gets a bit queasy and…"

Ruby seemed to lose interest in the doctor's tale at this juncture and slipped sideways off her chair, banging her head on the surgery grandfather clock as she fell.

"…tends to faint," concluded Len, looking heavenwards with a huge sigh.

The doctor rocketed up from his chair and rushed over to examine her.

"Oh dear me!" he winced. "She's had a nasty bump on the head! There'll be a duck-egg there in the morning."

He gently lifted her up and applied the smelling salts, just as he had done to David, and achieved the same dramatic results. Ruby rejoined the land of the living, and immediately asked the classic, if clichéd question, "Where am I?"

"Well, that *is* the whole family now," laughed the doctor. "How many fingers am I holding up, Mrs Day?"

"Sixteen."

"She'll be fine. She still has a sense of humour, that's the main thing. I'll spare you the gory details. David's fine, now that I've, erm, done something to his leg. Just take it easy till it heals, son. No football, no rough and tumble in the playground. I'll give you a note to keep you off games, if you need one."

Len stood up and gathered his battered troops together.

"Well, thank you very much, doctor…. Sorry, I don't know your name."

"Doctor Hoon."

David gave Mally a meaningful look.

"You're not from round here, judging by your accent."

"No, I'm from far, far away, but currently I'm in Tenbury Wells, or at least, that's my latest posting. I've spent my life whizzing all over the place, to be honest. Itchy feet, you see. Lord knows what my accent is nowadays. Martian probably!"

The doctor turned to grin at Mally, who he felt was being left out of things a little, what with one thing and another. Mally just stared blankly at him, with his mouth wide open.

"It's a good job the surgery wasn't officially open for business," continued the doctor, "or it really *would* have been chaos. I only popped in to catch up on a few things. I was about to go out when you hammered on the door."

"Do you know a strange woman in Tenbury Wells?" asked Mally, seemingly apropos of nothing.

"Which one?" asked the doctor, puzzled. "Most of them are strange there!"

"She lives near Newnham Bridge in a tiny cottage with a caravan next to it, and sells vegetables."

"Oh, her!" groaned the doctor, "How on earth do *you* know her? Don't get me started on that one. She regards me as her arch-enemy."

"I know, she told me," replied Mally.

The doctor looked hurt. He hadn't expected the woman to broadcast it to all and sundry. She seemed to be taking their herbal-versus-traditional medicine disagreement a little too personally.

"She said that her garlics would take over the world, and that they were very powerful," explained Mally, embroidering the tale a little for dramatic effect.

"Well, it's true that they have all sorts of powers," admitted the doctor, "but they'll never replace me, that's for sure. I bet they can't sew up a badly gashed leg, can they?"

Len glanced over at Ruby anxiously. She was still conscious.

"No, because they couldn't hold a needle with that robot arm or that rubber sucker thing," chipped in David. "But they could shoot you with their ray gun."

This seemed to plunge the good doctor into uncharted territory. He felt that he could add nothing worthwhile to the boy's latest remark, and therefore didn't. Maybe, he reflected, the lad was still in shock. He caught Len's eye with a quizzical look.

"Don't worry, doctor," Len assured him, "he speaks fluent gibberish, does our David. Now, we ought to leave you in peace, and thanks again."

"It's a pleasure, and I hope young Clive is okay. It's a little too early to say at the moment, but the hospital will phone me, I'm sure. And now, folks, if you don't mind, I'm going to have to fly!"

CHAPTER 7

That flat feeling

Thirty-five-year-old Len Day was busy gluing Mike Summerbee's legs to his football boots when his wife called him in for dinner. He'd taken the day off because his hand was heavily bandaged and sore, but even so, he hated to be sitting around doing nothing. He was interrupted by Mrs Homer, calling him from the garden fence. She just wanted to thank him for his help, and to tell everyone that the surgeon, Mr Patel, had succeeded in sewing the finger back on. Clive would never play the violin again, warned the doctor, but this was hardly a problem, as he never could in the first place. At least he'd be able to pick his nose. Len modestly accepted his praise and returned to Mike Summerbee, whose injury, had he been human and not made of plastic, would have taxed Mr Patel far more than a mere severed digit.

Meanwhile, half a mile away in the High Street, David, Mally and Gary were trudging towards Doctor Rodgerson's surgery to check out the latest Tardis sighting. Walking for any real distance was extremely uncomfortable for David, due to his stitches, and also for Gary, thanks to his gammy leg. He never complained, but knowing full well that he was on another wild-goose chase wasn't putting him in the best of moods. Out of breath after the steep incline, they arrived at the surgery.

"Where is it then?" asked Gary indignantly. "I can't see it."

"It's round the corner, right up against her waiting room window," explained Mally.

He marched around the corner.

"Only it's not," he sighed.

"What?" asked Gary indignantly. He looked for himself. There was a noticeable absence of time-travelling spacecraft.

"Are you two just making fun of me?" asked Gary, hurt.

"But I *swear* it was there," insisted David, ruffling his hair up, the way Stan Laurel often used to do when perplexed. "This proves that he's the real Doctor Who, as far as I'm concerned."

"Oh, right!" snapped Gary. "Not finding a police box proves Doctor Who really exists. That's like the vicar telling me he's never met God, or seen him, or spoken to him, or ever met anyone who ever has, so therefore he definitely flipping exists. I like that!"

"Yes, I agree on that one, but we did see the Tardis twice, which means that it wasn't just any old police box but a flying one. And another thing. Just examine the facts. I leave a garlic egg at Miss Kettle's. It turns into twelve robots. Fact! The police box arrives to deal with them. Fact! Then the box is parked outside the doctor's. Fact! The doctor isn't our usual one. It's Doctor Hoon. Fact! Ask my dad if you don't believe me, go on! It's obvious he's changed his name a bit to make it sound like an earth name. He'd got a long scarf on, and wild white hair, he knew the Strange Woman; he admitted he was from far away and whizzes about all over the place, and he also said he spoke fluent Martian. What more proof do you need?"

"Well it's funny how it's always you and Mally isn't it? How come I'm never there?"

"I don't know," replied an exasperated David, shaking his head. "Maybe you'll be there next time there's a sighting. Now let's get back before Mr Lewis gives us detention."

* * *

Mr Lewis was on the playing fields tending to the pitch in preparation for the cricket competition. The first of several house matches began in an hour's time, and the grass was still too long. He called for Mr Slavin, the caretaker, to run over it once more with the sit-on mower, and then to give the wicket itself a good rollering.

David and Gary hobbled over to say hello, and to ask if there was anything they could do to help. Mr Lewis thanked them and asked Gary to fetch the trophy from the cabinet in the hall. He slipped him the key, warning him to be careful with it. The cup was large, made of real silver with a black base, and very heavy indeed. It had been donated to the school when it first opened, and was engraved with the words 'Brierley Bank Junior School Cricket Cup'.

"Make sure you hang on to the base, or it might drop off," added Mr Lewis. "Hold it with both hands, and if it gets too heavy, have a rest. It would be a disaster if you dropped it and dented it. Right, David, you pop along to the grey metal

84

cabinet by the Head's study. Unlock it with this key and fetch me the megaphone, would you? In fact, fetch both of them. One is broken and sounds terrible, but I can't remember which one it is."

The two invalids hobbled off to do their chores and were back ten minutes later. Mr Lewis instructed Gary to place the cup on the trestle table where the glasses of orange squash were. He liked the children to see what they were playing for, in the hope that it would inspire them. The teacher took a megaphone from David and turned it on.

"Testing, one two, one two," he called. It was crackling terribly and distorting his lovely Welsh voice almost unrecognizably.

"Dear me!" he complained. "Give me the other one. He repeated the exercise and deemed the result satisfactory.

"I have to use this, or the little devils can't hear me," he explained.

"What shall I do with this one?" asked David, handing over the key.

"Chuck it in the bin, would you? It's hopeless. It hasn't worked right for ages."

David turned to return to the school in order to carry out his teacher's instructions, but stopped to watch Mr Slavin, who had swapped his sit-on mower for a manual roller. He was sweating and grunting his way along the wicket, doing his level best to turn Brierley Bank's dramatically undulating surface into something the cricketers could play on without the aid of a caddy. Gary was shuffling his way along the edge of the wicket and heading in the opposite direction towards the trestle table, struggling under the weight of the trophy. As the two crossed, Gary, with impeccable timing, tripped over Mr Slavin's discarded jumper and fell, hurling the cup onto the wicket.

There was a horrible inevitability about what happened next. David tried to call out, but his voice-box seemed to seize up, and everything appeared to be happening in slow motion. The mighty roller trundled over the silver cup, squashing it as flat as a pancake, and embedding it into the short grass of the wicket. Miraculously, the black base of the cup was unscathed, but this was of little consolation. The business end – the solid silver part, was now two-dimensional. Gary dragged himself to his knees and stared in disbelief at the damage he'd done. He began to sob brokenly and started to punch his bad leg. Mr Lewis dropped what he was doing and ran over to the disconsolate child, putting a fatherly arm around his shoulders and drying his eyes with a bit of screwed up tissue that he'd found in his track suit pocket.

"It was an accident, Gary," he whispered. "Don't you get upset about it. Am *I* getting upset?"

"N-n-n-n-no," Gary shuddered.

"Then *you* shouldn't be. Now why were you punching yourself? That's silly, isn't it?"

"It's my leg's fault. I'm always falling over. I'm useless."

Mr Lewis looked stern. "Don't you *ever* let me hear you say that again. You are one of my best pupils. My favourite pupils, as it happens. Now get yourself up, and dry your eyes. It's about time we had a new trophy. That one's a hundred years old if it's a day. Time it was retired, I say. Put out to grass. Oh, I see it has been already! That's better lad. Nice to see you smile!"

David hobbled towards them to see what was going on. His teacher gave him a wink and called him over.

"Look after Gary, will you? He's a bit upset."

"I don't know!" smiled David, ruffling up his friend's hair. "Wonky Legs United aren't we? I'm glad it was you, 'cause it's usually me!"

Mr Lewis gave David another wink. "David, we're sick of that heavy old thing - aren't we, Gary? We decided to flatten it in protest – be a love and pop back to the hall. This year we're playing for a new cup – The Brierley Bank Junior School Football Cup. Okay, it isn't quite right for a cricket competition, but if no-one looks too close at the engraving, they'll be none the wiser. No, wait a minute! That one's just as heavy. Fetch the Music Cup instead. That's the small one you won last year for best recorder solo in the Dudley Schools Competition. It's half the weight of the other two, and we don't want any more accidents. Off you trot, lad, or should I say limp. Take your time!"

The two teams of players, Red and Blue Houses, were filing out onto the pitch now, tossing cork balls to each other and practising their cover drives as they walked, like the professional s did. Mr Lewis donned his umpire's cow-gown and quickly consoled the other umpire, poor old Mr Slavin, who, whilst not actually sobbing, nevertheless was going through his own private grieving process. He had polished the Cricket and Football Cups – the oldest and most prestigious ones the school owned – for most of his working life. This was, for him, an especially sad day.

Once Mr Lewis had frisked him and removed all sharp objects and his box of aspirins, just in case, he turned to greet the two teams, calling the captains together for the toss. Blue team won, and elected to bat.

Meanwhile, David reappeared with the considerably lighter Music Cup, and placed it on the trestle table, so that the game could commence. He then climbed the bank to join Gary – whose mood had improved marginally – and manned the scoreboard.

After an exciting two hours, which helped take Gary's mind off things, Blue House won by a slender five runs, thanks in no small part to a heroic 'twenty-six not out' from Mally. After the celebrations had died down, everyone traipsed back across the pitch to the school changing rooms, carrying wickets, pads and bats. Gary shuffled off to meet his father, who was picking him up in the car after the game, and David busied himself with dismantling the scoreboard, unaware that his teacher was standing behind him.

"David, thank you for helping to lighten things earlier on with your little joke. Poor old Gary does get upset with himself occasionally, because of his leg. I can see you're struggling today after your nasty accident too. I never realized how bad it was until Malcolm mentioned it just after the game. I wouldn't have asked you to keep traipsing over to the hall if I'd known it was that bad. He reckons your knee bone was hanging out and there was a piece of flesh the size of a fillet steak hanging off a rusty nail!"

"Mally exaggerates, sir, but it was pretty bad. I daren't look at it or I might faint again, and my mother's keeled over three times already. The thing is, this'll heal up eventually, but Gary has to put up with his leg for life, doesn't he?"

"Afraid so, David."

Mr Lewis sensed the conversation needed lightening. He produced the flattened cup from his bag and begun to laugh.

"I know I shouldn't," he said, "but it is sort of funny isn't it? It's the kind of thing Laurel and Hardy would do. You can drop this in the bin with the megaphone. It's no use to anyone now."

"Can I keep it, sir?" asked David. "I could ask my dad if he could straighten it out a bit, and we could have it for our Subbuteo tournaments."

"I think it's beyond redemption to be honest, lad, but he's welcome to try. I'll have to persuade Mr Perriman to invest in a new one, and I'll insist it's a lighter one as well. If the cricket captain tried to lift this aloft after a victory, it would give him a hernia. It would have been better suited as a weight-lifting trophy, I reckon. At least the recipient could manage it! Take it, but you'll look a bit silly playing table football for a flattened cricket trophy, won't you?"

"I'll scratch out the word cricket and write Subbuteo F.A. Cup on it with one of my dad's engraving tools. Anyway, it's no sillier than cricketers playing for a music cup, sir."

"Point taken. It's all yours!"

* * *

On Monday evening, a fly on the wall of Len's tool shed would have observed its eponymous owner labouring over a task that would have got the better of lesser men. Whoever had flattened the trophy had done a very good job. Len doubted that the Luftwaffe could have done better. It was, as flat trophies went, a prime example. He set about easing the sides away from each other with chisel, followed by a padded iron bar for starters. After that, he'd try a bit of subtle panel beating. A wry smile formed on his lips as he pondered the amount of free time he spend engaged in these foolish, pointless exercises – usually at the behest of his dreamy son. He'd probably wasted his own father's time in exactly the same way. It was what free time was intended for, and what dads did.

A few yards away in the Day family living room, David was doing his best to remain civil. He was hosting a home Subbuteo fixture against Leeds United, otherwise known as Brett Spittle.

Had Ruby, as an experiment, trotted out of her kitchen and placed a huge dollop of any proprietary brand of best butter, without warning, into the slit-eyed, pug-faced little ogre's mouth and stood around in anticipation, she would have still been there at bedtime waiting for it to melt, such was his overly-polite attitude and sycophantic fawning.

"Thank you very much for my biscuit, Mrs Day. Shall I leave my muddy shoes in the hallway, Mrs Day?" he grovelled, but it didn't cut any ice with Ruby. She would quite like to have removed the laces from his muddy boots and throttled him with them, but, with admirable resolve, she said nothing. Brett was Doctor Jekyll while she was present, but unfortunately, he quickly became Mr Hyde when she departed, reminding his quivering opponent that he was known as a bad loser. Thankfully, David had moral support in the form of Gary, who had been asked along to referee the match. The newly formed league's founder, Robert Glazier, a stickler for rules and regulations, insisted that matches would be considered null and void unless an adjudicator was present. Luckily, he hadn't been quite so precise about the neutrality aspects. David had already experienced the effect that a partisan crowd could have on a result, and had wisely decided that two could play that particular game. Unfortunately, Mally had declined the invitation due to the fact that he had a thrush to stuff in a hurry. His mother had warned him that if it sent her Carnation milk off, there'd be hell to pay, so he needed to remove it from her fridge before she went on the warpath.

It was obvious to even the casual observer that Gary was cut out to be a referee. He had devoured the rule book and was applying the letter of the law, much to Brett's dissatisfaction. In the first half alone, Brett was warned about foul language, dissent and time wasting. He had had numerous free kicks and penalties awarded against him, some of which David had managed to convert, which meant that at the half-time whistle, the score read:

Manchester City – Twelve, Leeds United -Two.

To say that Brett's half-time biscuit wasn't going down well was an understatement. He was almost apoplectic with rage, but felt powerless to act, due to the fact that Mrs Day was hovering but a few feet away in the kitchen. Nor did he fare better in the second half. There are some athletes for whom a bit of rage is a good thing. It drives them on and makes them determined - it gives them an edge. Unfortunately, the opposite was true for Brett. He became bitter and twisted. His flicking finger stiffened, his face began to resemble a beetroot with high blood pressure, and he was beginning to dribble – a skill noticeably lacking in his players.

Gary's thirteenth penalty decision was the one that finally pushed Brett over the edge. Sweeping his hand across the baize, he scattered the twenty-two footballers to all corners of the living room and declared that he'd had enough. David hastily collected the Leeds players up and placed them back in Brett's box, ever the peacemaker.

"Sorry," he whispered. "Well played though. It was a closer game than the score….."

"I'll get you for this!"

David, still trying desperately to pour oil over troubled waters, saw Brett to the door.

"You'll probably win the return match at your house easily, I should think."

He opened the door and handed Brett his Leeds United box. Brett snatched it from him, and gestured for David to follow him.

"Look at that!" he whispered, pointing at the sky.

"What?" asked David, curious. There was talk of a meteorite storm in the newspapers.

"This!" snarled Brett, punching David in the eye, before running down the path and into the night.

David began to wail, which brought his mother dashing to the door, closely followed by Gary. She took him back inside and examined his injury. A big, red weal had started to form under his eye, and tears were streaming down his face.

"What on earth happened?" she asked, applying a cold flannel.

"I, erm, t-t-turned around after saying goodbye to Brett, and walked into the door," David lied.

Gary gave him a look that suggested he believed otherwise.

"I don't know," said Ruby. "You are the most accident-prone child I know. Gashed knees, black eyes. What next?"

David sat down in the living room, his eye running and blinking furiously, while Gary helped tidy up and put the pitch away.

"He pailed you didn't he?"

"Yes, but don't tell mom. She confronts Brett's mother, and it just makes things worse."

"I know, but you can't just let him get away with it."

"I'm not going to. My dad always says, revenge is a dish eaten cold."

"What's that mean?"

"Dunno!"

"It sounds daft to me," frowned Gary. "You can't eat a dish, for a start. It would break your teeth."

"I think that's what it means. If you want revenge, make them eat a dish and it'll break their teeth off."

"Still doesn't sound right."

"Well, whatever it means, dad said sometimes you don't have to hit someone to get revenge. If you're no good at fighting, you can do it a different way. He reckons it's best to do it later on, after they've forgotten all about it and they're not expecting it. That's what I'm going to do."

"How?"

"Dunno. I'll think about it."

Len burst into the living room holding the silver cup and was greeted by doom and gloom.

"What's going on here?" he asked, concerned.

"David walked into the door, Mr Day, that's all," explained Gary.

"Well, this'll help cheer you up. The Brierley Bank Subbuteo F.A. Cup, as good as new, if you look at it from down the garden in the dark without your glasses on."

CHAPTER 8

Brett's Achilles Heel

It was a beautiful Saturday afternoon and David was returning from a visit to his grandparents' house. By his standards, it had been a fairly quiet week at school, in that there had been no new Tardis sightings, Brett hadn't hit him again and there were no more robots in Miss Kettle's window. He'd played another Subbuteo league match against Mally, of all people, which resulted in an honourable six-all draw, after which David had mooted the idea of the F.A. Cup competition to Robert Glazier. To his surprise and delight, Master Glazier had been extremely enthused, especially with the promise of an impressive real silver trophy - which he hoped to win himself - and had immediately set about organizing things. David had also remembered to ask if it was okay for new teams to enter, which Glazier agreed to as long as each team paid a shilling stake to take part. That way, the eventual winner (which was almost certainly going to be Robert Glazier) would have a cash prize *and* a trophy.

And so it was that David skipped down the High Street in his Fair-Isle jumper and balaclava whistling a jaunty tune, seemingly without a care in the world, for a change. As he passed the church, he saw the vicar chatting to a young couple, and politely wished him good morning.

"Ah, good morning!" replied the vicar, making his excuses to the couple, who were running late anyway. "I'm pleased it's you. I've been delving into the parish records, trying to find our Mr Silversmith, and guess what?"

"He doesn't exist?"

"How did you know that?"

"My friend's dad told me. He's in a local history society."

"He's quite correct. It's all very strange, don't you think?"

"Yes. And there's some treasure buried somewhere that no-one will ever find now."

"True, unless we can locate pieces of this man's furniture locally, of course. If he was a carpenter by trade, surely his work would still be in evidence around the town. Maybe he even carved them with his initials. I was thinking we could place an advertisement in the Express and Star newspaper to try and find examples of his work. I would bet a hundred pounds that he's hidden his money in a chest of drawers, a table or a wardrobe, even a grandfather clock. There'll be a secret compartment built into it, mark my words. I'll have a chat to Mr Lewis, and see if he thinks it's worth the trouble. Remember, if the treasure *is* found, by rights a portion of it belongs to you boys. Finders keepers, eh? The owner of the furniture, would, of course expect a generous cut too. Mind you, a donation to the church would be nice, as it was on our property!"

David tactfully reminded the excited vicar that currently, no-one knew where the furniture in question was, if it indeed existed at all, so it was a little premature to start counting chickens and distributing hypothetical wealth. His mother and father were always doing that, and it always led to frustration. They'd have heated disagreements about how they were to spend the premium bonds prize they hadn't actually won yet, and both would end up sulking. Len would want to spend it on a new car, and Ruby a holiday in Devon. It was only when their little boy pointed out the obvious flaw in their plans that they began to see sense.

David bade the vicar farewell and continued on his journey. It was just as he rounded the corner, not far from Brett Spittle's unkempt and unloved house that something stopped him in his tracks, causing his heart to leap into his mouth in search of an emergency exit. Blocking half of the footpath directly in front of him was the elusive blue police box, and emerging from it was the doctor, dressed in a long flowing scarf and a fedora hat. David knew that he wanted to find Gary immediately and show him the proof, but for some reason, his limbs just wouldn't work. He just stood there, gawping, until finally his weedy legs spun him around and began to run, whipping back and forth like two pieces of knotted string, in the general direction of Gary's house.

Thankfully, they didn't have too far to go. Gary's parents lived just behind the High Street in a little terraced house, and David was able to reach his destination, winded and breathless, in under two minutes. Summoning his last ounce of strength, he wheezed "GA –REEEE!" and in due course, Gary appeared. He was clad in a tartan dressing gown and was wearing red slippers, having just come downstairs from his bi-annual bath.

"The police box is back again, and it's just round the corner from here!" yelled David.

"I'll get dressed!" replied Gary.

"No time," insisted David. He'd cried wolf twice already, and he couldn't face Gary giving him that hurt look for the third time. "Come on, you'll do. One quick look and you can be back home in five minutes."

Gary shuffled out and followed his friend down the street, as amused onlookers looked on, amused. Brierley Bank had always been a fairly eccentric town, but a stick insect in a balaclava pursued by a limping lad in his dressing gown and underwear was still an unusual sight on a Saturday afternoon. As they rounded the corner into the High Street, David breathed a huge sigh of relief and turned to his struggling comrade. The police box - glory be! – was still there. Gary, who had got a bad case of the stitch, divided his time between gazing in amazement and doubling up in agony. The doctor was still standing next to the box, but now he was chatting to a couple of workmen in donkey jackets. He broke off from his conversation to address David.

"Ah, Master Day, unless I am mistaken. How's the leg? It doesn't seem to have affected your running ability, I'm pleased to say, but I am worried about our doctor-patient relationship. You took one look at me earlier and ran off, you devil. I know I gave you a hard time with those stitches, but it wasn't personal!"

David stood there, panting like a Labrador after a long walk on a hot day.

"And who's your scantily-clad accomplice? Do all the kids around here lie in on a Saturday till three?"

98

Gary finally caught up with David and stood in reverence, studying the apparition before him.

"Are you Doctor Who?" he asked.

"Doctor *who*?" replied the doctor, smiling mischievously.

"Doctor Who, off the telly?"

The good doctor doubled up with laughter. The two workmen whom he had been chatting to did likewise.

"You really thought I was Doctor Who? Oh, I see, stepping out of the Tardis; the scarf and hat. And my name! Oh, that's priceless, it really is!"

"Does that mean you're not then?"

"I wish I could say yes, lads, but alas, I'm just plain old Doctor Hoon, which I admit is similar."

"So why are you in the police box?" asked Gary, scratching his head in a deflated kind of way.

"Oh, I see. Well, these men were just finishing off the cabling, and I've never had a look inside one of these before, so I asked if I could take a peek."

"But that doesn't explain why it keeps disappearing and turning up somewhere else," argued Gary.

"Ah! I can explain that," said one of the workmen, still highly amused at the misunderstanding. "We assembled the thing by Miss Kettle's place initially, but that's a bad bend, and the Gardner's pop lorry demolished it. Turns out the bloke in charge of the pop lorry preferred Banks's Mild to pop. Our boss thought it best to site the replacement lower down by the surgery, but Doctor Rodgerson played up, because she said it blocked out all her light, and you know what she's like. She says jump, and you ask, how high? So we've ended up putting it here, and so far - touch wood - nobody's objected. Mind you, it is early days."

"But what about the Strange Woman?" asked David, deflated. "The woman from Tenbury."

"What's she got to do with it?" asked the doctor, puzzled.

"She breeds garlics, which turn into robots. I left a garlic egg at Miss Kettle's shop, and the next day there were twelve baby robots in her window."

The laughter that emanated from Doctor Hoon upon discovering that the boys thought he was a Time Lord was nothing to the laughter that burst from his quivering frame now. It was a full two minutes before he could manage to speak again – two minutes of sheer embarrassment for David, who was notoriously thin-skinned.

"David, my dear child, the things that woman sells are garlics. The robots on Doctor Who are called Daleks. Have you never watched it?"

"No, we don't have a telly, but Brett Spittle said they were real, and he's seen them."

"Well, I'm sorry to be the bearer of bad news, but the programme isn't a documentary, it's fiction. I couldn't explain what the little Daleks were doing in Miss Kettle's window, but they've got nothing to do with garlic. That's just a plant. It's used in cooking, and some people think it's got medicinal qualities too."

"But why did you say it was very powerful?"

"Ah! I see where we're going now. It *is* powerful. Just half a clove – that's what they call the pods inside – is strong enough to flavour a whole pot of stew, and if you were to eat one raw, you'd smell to high heaven the next day. That's what was meant by powerful. If you swallowed all twelve, you'd stink so badly, no-one would come near you!"

"Really?" asked David.

"Really, so you see. They are powerful, in their own way. Now I must go. I'm holding these people up, and don't forget, I need to see you to remove the stitches at some point soon. Your mate here seems as if he's got a stitch too, but I can't remove his, unfortunately. Hard to run when the polio's affected your leg, eh son?"

Gary nodded.

"I'm sorry you've had to endure it, but we doctors are trying our best to stamp it out. Be assured of that."

And with that, the Time Lord disappeared down the High Street, his Hereford United Football Club scarf flowing behind him.

David and Gary gave each other a look that said it all. They were feeling extremely foolish, Gary even more so, because he was still clad in his dressing gown at three in the afternoon. They wandered down the High Street and paused at Miss Kettle's, just as a spivvy-looking gent with a pencil moustache and dressed in a brown tweed three-piece suit was leaving.

"Thank you, Miss Kettle," he called, doffing his hat. "I told you them Daleks would sell well, didn't I? It's 'cause of the telly, see. Mind you, I didn't expect all twelve to sell in one foul sweep! Fancy having twelve kids in this day and age. I ask yer! I bet that's why she insisted her old man bought a telly!"

David and Gary paused to look in the window, as they always did. Twelve more miniature Daleks stood, guarding the shop, their ray guns at the ready.

"Huh!" sighed David.

"Oh well!" added Gary.

They reached the hardware store, where Mrs Edith Spittle was chatting to her mother, Gloria, in the doorway. As David hurried past her, she said something that stopped him in his tracks. He pretended to study the Swiss army knife in the window, the better to overhear their conversation, gesturing to Gary to do likewise.

"Our Brett won't watch it," said Mrs Spittle. "He's scared stiff of 'em."

"Stupid fool!" replied his sympathetic and caring grandmother. "Doesn't he realize it ain't real?"

"He hides behind the settee if they start talking, shaking like a leaf. For one as is so tough - or likes to think he is - he's a right pansy when they come on. Mind you, if I told his mates about it, he'd go mad. You should have seen the hate in his eyes when I had him on about telling Shaun. I thought he was gonna take a swing at me, small as he is! I just shouted 'Exterminate!' at him, and he went white."

David had heard enough. He slipped around the corner and the two headed for Gary's house. Deep inside his head, a plan was formulating. Brett was soon going to be shattering his nasty little milk teeth on a cold dish.

CHAPTER 9

Len gets cracking

"Dad," said David sheepishly.

"What?" replied Len, chewing a mouthful of smoked haddock. He could always tell by the way David said 'dad' that he was about to drop some bombshell or other.

"Dad, could you build me a Dalek by Wednesday night?"

"If I knew what a Dalek was, I might be able to."

"It's a sort of robot."

"I see."

"The robots that are on Doctor Who, which you've never seen because we don't have a telly."

"Ah right! That old chestnut again. And why do you need a robot?"

"Erm, because everybody is mad about Doctor Who and we like to play it in the playground, so Mr Lewis said we could write a play about time travel and he asked if anyone's dad was good at building stuff, and I said mine was, and he

said can you ask him to build a Dalek for our play, and I said
I would and……"

"David, why do you always volunteer me for everything?
Remember the Nativity play? Guess who was lumbered with
building the stable? Muggins here. When you did the panto,
who was it who had to make the royal carriage out of
hardboard? Guess who? Are there no other dads in Brierley
Bank who know which way round to hold a screwdriver?"

"Sorry, dad."

"I don't even know what a flipping Dalek looks like, for
starters."

"I could draw you one with my thirteen-colour biro."

"And why Wednesday night? That doesn't give me much
time you know."

"Sorry, dad. I'll help. It's so we can have a rehearsal after
school."

Len sighed a deep sigh. He could have said no, of course.
Most dads would have done, but there was something about
the look on his adored son's stupid little face that wouldn't
let him. He'd planned to put his feet up on Sunday, after a
hard week in the tool shop. What he really didn't need was a
day and two evenings building a robot in a cold shed.

"What colour are they? I can't do painting. I'm hopeless at
it. You can do that."

"Agreed! All we need is the basic construction. Me, Mally
and Gary will finish it off."

"Okay, but I want a working drawing as soon as possible,
and please, I don't want any help with constructing it. Just

104

leave me alone and it'll be done twice as quick. Start drawing!"

"Okay, dad. Thank you!" David beamed. "Just one quick thing, before I start. Did you say that Uncle Bill worked for the Express and Star?"

"Yes, why?"

"The vicar wants to get an article published about Jeremiah Silversmith, asking if anyone owns a piece of his furniture. He was a Victorian carpenter you see, so there might just be someone who still has one of his cabinets or whatever. We're trying to find his hidden treasure, and the vicar says me, Gary and Mally are entitled to a share if we ever find it."

"That'll be like trying to find a needle in a haystack. Besides, Bill is a type compositor, not a reporter. He sets the type for the pages, that's all."

"Yes, but I bet he could tell us who to contact, couldn't he?"

"I would have thought so," said Len. "Go and ask him while it's still light – once you've drawn a Dalek for me."

* * *

Half an hour later, David was showing his father the Dalek drawing and trying to explain the finer points, which was proving difficult, as he'd only ever seen a miniature one.

"I think this is how they look, but obviously, they're about five feet tall. The ray gun will need to wiggle about, and we need space inside it for one of us to stand. They just sort of glide about I think, just like Miss Kettle does."

105

Len shook his head in despair. "Look, David, I'd love to help you, but this isn't accurate enough for me. It doesn't help that you've never actually seen one yourself."

David's bottom lip curled, but after a few seconds of deep thought, a light bulb flickered to life somewhere in his head. "I know - you could have a walk up the High Street and see the ones in Miss Kettle's window. They're small, but they look really realistic. Why not buy one and copy it?"

"Right."

"And then I could play with it afterwards."

"How much are these blessed things?"

"Not much."

"Go on then, but I'm far too daft with you! I could do with a bit of fresh air, if the air in the High Street could ever be described as fresh. If you pop along to your Uncle Bill's, he's actually got a telly. Ask nicely and he might let you watch the programme. It's on on Saturdays isn't it?"

"I think so. That's a brilliant idea!" said David, dashing for the outhouse door. "Thanks dad!"

Len slipped his shoes on, wondering to himself if Jeremiah the miserly carpenter would have put himself out to make a robot for a persistent child. Somehow, he very much doubted it.

* * *

David returned from his Uncle Bill's at seven, and was delighted to find his dad already at work down the shed, measuring a tiny Dalek and working out the proportions.

106

"I'm going to construct the base section out of deal, and screw some castors on the bottom so it appears to glide," he enthused. "If we double up that old roll of black rubber, it'll do for the bumping car buffer thingy at the bottom, and it'll also be handy for covering up the castors. Then I can cut sheets of hardboard to size and nail them onto the frame for the panels. The head section is the trickiest, but I reckon I can use quarter inch ply and cut those bits out with a fret saw. They'll slot onto a frame nicely, and we can fix this black mesh inside so you can't see the person operating it."

David smiled. His dad always did this. Initially, he'd moan about the latest challenge that he'd been set by his demanding offspring, but when he got started, he became obsessed, and couldn't bear to cut corners.

"The bobbles on these panels are difficult to construct, I must admit," Len stroked his sandpaper-like chin in thought. "No, wait! I've got a box full of clay pigeons from down the caravan. Do you remember when we spent all afternoon collecting up the ones no-one had hit? I can glue them on in rows, and they'll be perfect. Now all we need is a ray gun, an eye and that thing that resembles a sink plunger."

"Why don't we use mom's sink plunger for that bit?" asked David.

"Perfect! Why didn't I think of that? Don't worry about the other bits. I'll soon sort those out. How did you get on with Uncle Bill?"

"Oh, great. He's helping me with the newspaper thing, and we watched Doctor Who. I saw a real Dalek, and now I know what they talk like and how they move and everything!"

"Good. Now hand me that ping-pong ball. I've had a great idea for that eyeball on a stick."

* * *

By Sunday evening, Len was exhausted, but the Dalek was virtually complete, except for a few finishing touches and, of course, the paint job. The castors made it extremely manoeuvrable in spite of its weight, and Len had made the head section detachable so that a little boy could slip inside.

"I hope your Mr Lewis appreciates me," he sighed, as he slumped into his favourite armchair to savour what little of Sunday he had left. Before long, sleep had engulfed his tired frame and he began to snore gently, much to Ruby's annoyance. It was only half past nine, and she hadn't seen him all day.

* * *

Traditionally, Ruby Day spent Mondays ironing, but after some fairly impressive pleading from David, she reluctantly agreed to spend the day undercoating the Dalek. Her Aunt Millie had called at the house at eleven, with a view to popping up the High Street to visit Bertha and Reuben for a cup of tea and a slice of bread pudding – something Ruby would usually have jumped at – and was somewhat nonplussed when her niece informed her that she couldn't, because she was undercoating a Dalek. It was the first time Ruby had ever used that sentence, and it was unlikely that it would ever be employed again. She watched through the net curtains as Millie left the cul-de-sac a dejected woman, and returned to her duties, convinced that she, Mrs Ruby Day – previously of sound mind and body - was very slowly going mad, largely due to ten years of motherhood. Would other parents around the estate have spent all day painting their son's life-sized Daleks? She didn't think so!

* * *

At lunchtime, David made his excuses and ran up to Miss Kettle's shop. He was dreading the encounter, because the ogre was unpleasant even when he was parting with his hard-earned cash. Asking a favour could potentially send the woman over the edge into physical violence, or at the very least turn the air in the shop blue.

He swallowed his Adam's apple and made a loud gulping noise – an action that did not help in the least to fortify him against what he felt sure was about to happen. He entered the shop, setting off the tinkling bell above the door, and seconds later, the diminutive Miss Kettle, dressed, like Hamlet, in her customary suit of black, glided in like a particularly malevolent and wrinkly human Dalek.

"What?" she asked, for here was a lady who gave words away like they cost her a penny each.

"Erm, sorry to bother you, but did I leave a small package wrapped in tissue here, a few days ago?"

"Yes."

"Erm, have you still - you know - got it?"

"Yes."

"Oh, good. It didn't hatch out into twelve baby robots then?"

Miss Kettle stared at him. The effect was broadly similar to standing before the black leader Dalek and being slowly frazzled by its ray gun. David gulped again, and pressed on.

"Is there any chance I could have it back, please, only it's important?"

"Yes." She glided back into her sitting room and returned a minute later with the garlic bulb, which she handed over.

David's face lit up. "Thank you, oh thank you very much!"

He skipped out of the shop, and had the fly on the wall that had earlier been present in Len's shed now been assigned to covering the action in Miss Kettle's shop, it would have sworn that it witnessed the merest hint of a softening around the edges of the old curmudgeon's lips. The fly, were it an honest fly, would not have gone as far as describing what it saw as a smile, but the signs were encouraging.

CHAPTER 10

The Sting

Mally was dreading tomorrow coming. He had known for some time that Wednesday was the day West Bromwich Albion played Leeds United at home, and he feared crowd trouble. The fixture against Manchester City had ended in violence, and he didn't want a repeat of that happening around his house, thank you very much. Leeds United was fast gaining a reputation for crowd violence, and it was ruining the beautiful game. Mally's parents had been forewarned, however, which helped, but then David had outlined a scheme which had made the bristly hairs on the back of Mally's neck – the result of a recent visit to Freddie Fielding's Barber Shop – stand on end, like quills on the fretful porpentine, as Shakespeare once put it.

Mally loved David like a brother, but David could be quietly determined sometimes, and when he got that bit between his teeth, there was little Mally could do to stop him. This latest scheme, even by David's standards, was a corker. Thankfully, there was quite a lot going on at school to take his mind off things a little. Mr Lewis had been approached by an Express and Star reporter, thanks to Uncle

Bill's efforts, and the newspaper had agreed to run an article asking for anyone owning a piece of furniture either carved or constructed by one Jeremiah Silversmith to contact the editor. No mention was made of the reason for the enquiry, but it was hinted that the piece might have a value. The article also requested that those who had heard of the man, or had any archival evidence that he even existed, should get in touch. Much to his embarrassment, Mr Lewis was persuaded to be photographed looking suitably puzzled and standing next to Jeremiah's grave. The article was scheduled to appear that very evening, if the reporter could post his copy in time. Feedback from Express and Star articles was usually very good, he assured the teacher, and he confidently predicted that the mystery would be solved by the weekend.

The cricket cup was also in full swing, with the house teams batting their socks off to secure the coveted ten inch high Music Trophy. Size, they were reminded by Mr Lewis, was not everything. The famous Ashes urn, after all, was even smaller, at a mere four and a half inches.

On the Subbuteo front, league matches were being played left, right and centre all across Brierley Bank, thanks in no small part to the efficiency of Robert Glazier, or Aston Villa, as he was also known. He had also got back to David vis-a-vis his mooted F.A. Cup competition, and even drawn the first round from a hat. Gary had entered as Brierley Bank Celtic, causing loud guffaws from those present when the draw was made.

"I chose them especially," he argued, above the laughter, "because when I came last, I wanted it to be the team's fault, not mine!"

Robert Glazier cared not who entered, just as long as they coughed up their shilling. As hot favourite, it was a case of the more entrants the better. He just drew the line at girls.

Gary was drawn at home for his first round tie, against Crystal Palace, a freckle-faced little half-pint named Derek Batham, who looked as if he'd been sunbathing with a colander over his face. This fixture was causing a fair bit of consternation, as Brierley Bank still didn't possess a pitch and the board of directors – Gary's parents – weren't made of money. Luckily, David had other plans on Wednesday, and Maine Road was available for hire, free of charge, if Gary could pop by and collect it.

Thanks to Ruby's sterling effort with the undercoat, David had been able to spend Tuesday glossing the Dalek, which now looked menacing and magnificent, and, coincidentally, matched the front door exactly. By Wednesday teatime, it was dry and ready for action.

"Shall I run you up to the school with it?" asked Len, as the three stood admiring their handiwork.

"Erm, no, no, it's okay," spluttered David, "I, erm, fancy pushing it through the street, just for a laugh! Gary'll be here soon for the Subbuteo pitch. He'll help me."

"I know, but really…" protested Len.

"Leave them have a bit of fun with it," interrupted Ruby. "Don't you remember when you were a kid? They'll be okay."

Len reluctantly acquiesced, and David offered a silent prayer to whoever was up there, watching over him.

Gary arrived seconds later, and stood in awe, gazing at what the Days had created. David glided the monster out of the outhouse door, impressed by its manoeuvrability and handling, and was about to set off with his friend when he suddenly stopped, whacked his brow with his palm, and shot back upstairs to his bedroom. He emerged again with a large plastic carrier bag containing the football pitch for Gary, and the two set off along the cul-de-sac with their sinister friend.

Len smiled and turned to his wife, who was still liberally plastered in battleship grey undercoat.

"I dunno. Kids, eh?" he said, shaking his head in disbelief. "Still, that gives us an hour to ourselves, I suppose. Why don't we go and wash that paint off?"

* * *

Pushing the Dalek up the hill had been hard work, and David was pleased that Gary was there to help. It was just a shame that he was going to miss the adventure. They rolled on until they reached Doctor Rodgerson's surgery, pausing for a breather where the blue police box had been. Inside, they could see Doctor Hoon standing in the empty waiting room, so David cheekily tapped the window and ducked down. The doctor turned quickly, and was suddenly face to face with a malevolent-looking red Dalek who was eyeing him up and down with his ping pong ball. The effect on the poor doctor was electric. He could think of no earthly reason why this was happening to him, and he looked as if he'd seen a ghost. Was he going crazy, he wondered? Was the strain of looking after Doctor Rodgerson's surgery single-handedly proving too much? He looked again, but the robot had gone. Maybe, heaven forbid, those schoolboys had been right after all, and Daleks were indeed invading Brierley

Bank. He was sure there was some logical explanation, but he could think of none offhand. Doctor Hoon strode to the door and walked through the corridor to the front entrance. He opened the door and scanned the High Street up and down, but there was no-one in sight, other than an old lady walking her Staffordshire bull terrier and two chainmakers leaving the chain shop for home after a hard day. He staggered back into the surgery, running his liver-spotted great hands through his wild white hair. What he needed at this precise moment, more than anything, was a large glass of Scotch.

* * *

David and Gary emerged from the alley and said their goodbyes. David handed his friend the green baize pitch and goalposts, wishing him good luck for his first ever game. It was but a short step to Mally's house now, and he could just about manage the Dalek and the carrier bag on his own.

Once outside the house, David called for his friend, who opened the door to a sight he would never forget. He walked out slowly, circumnavigating Len's magnificent creation, and admiring it from every angle. David explained how the head came off, to enable a child to sit inside and operate the three protruding sticks, which he referred to as the eyeball, plunger and ray gun. Then he showed Mally the pièce-de-résistance. By clicking the switch within, two small lights on top of the head came on, and a red light began to flash on and off at the end of the ray gun.

"I can't believe it!" gasped Mally, awestruck. "It's just like a real one. Did you bring the other things?"

"Yes," David assured him. "We're all ready to go. Help me through the house with it, and let's have a test run before he turns up."

* * *

Brett rang the doorbell at six-thirty, and was let in by Mrs Stevens.

"Malcolm is waiting for you in the living room," she smiled, through gritted teeth. "Are you going to have some tea with us before you play?"

"Yes," replied Brett. "What is it?"

"Fish fingers, peas and mashed potatoes," said Mrs Stevens. "Is that alright with you?"

"I like loads of mash," said Brett.

"Please!" whispered Mrs Stevens to no-one in particular, as she waltzed back into the kitchen.

The two opponents sat at the kitchen table, quietly eating their food.

"I don't like this mash much," announced Brett. "It's not as good as my mother's, and hers isn't that good. It tastes horrible."

"Well, you've eaten most of it anyway," said Mrs Stevens tartly. She had never had the pleasure of meeting Brett Spittle before, but she had been warned about him. All of a sudden, she was beginning to appreciate David and Gary. Both of them always said 'please' and 'thank you', for starters.

After tea, Mally returned to the sitting room, where his Subbuteo pitch was laid out, and invited Brett to place his players in position. Mally's father was sat on the settee, reading the Express and Star.

"My God!" he cried suddenly. "Have you seen this, lads?"

He showed them the cover story. In large, bold letters, it read:

DALEK INVASION

BRIERLEY BANK POLICE PUT ON ALERT

Sightings of the deadly robots in Black Country

cause widespread panic.

Brett's centre forward dropped from his paralysed fingers. He stared incredulously at the newspaper, seemingly unable to speak.

"But I thought Doctor Who was just a story," said Mally, hamming it up for all he was worth.

"Oh no," replied his father, biting his lip to fend off a giggling fit. "No, a lot of people think that. The series on telly was based on real-life events. If they *have* invaded Brierley Bank, as it says here, this is deadly serious. We'd better lock all the doors, just in case."

Any amateur psychologist could have worked out what was happening inside Brett's head at a glance. The usually guarded little thug appeared to be wearing his heart on his sleeve. His friend, the similarly bullet-headed Kenny Higgs had categorically assured him that Daleks were definitely real, but Brett had been in two minds. He was neither a believer nor a disbeliever. Where Daleks were concerned, he sat on the fence – a Dalek agnostic, if you will. Now Mally's father was showing him the cover of a well-respected local newspaper that *proved* his friend had been correct. After all, newspapers did not lie. If the Star said that Daleks were invading Earth, then invading Earth they jolly well were. It was very soon after this catastrophic information had been fully digested that another emotion contorted Brett's face – namely, blind panic. He tried to act nonchalantly, but it was all too obvious that this bombshell had got in amongst him and given the lad a good shaking. He began to arrange his players, by way of taking his mind off things, but his hands trembled, and his team formation (one-one-eight) was so bizarre that it was worthy of an England manager.

"Er, does it s-say where they've spotted the Daleks?" he asked shakily.

Mally's father held himself together with an almighty effort.

"Hang on, let me read…..oh dear me! They've been sighted all over Brierley Bank. A lady returning home with her shopping saw a spaceship land on Mary Stevens Park, and more than fifty Daleks got out, scattering in all directions."

"Oh no!"

"Anyway, lads, let's not get *too* worried. We should be safe here. After all, why would they want to get us?

"D-d-dunno!" replied Brett, the colour draining from his ferret features.

118

"Come on then. Let's get the game underway. I'll be referee, being as Gary couldn't make it."

Mally kicked off, trying not to make eye contact with his dad for fear of cracking up. He flicked an expert pass to his striker, and shuffled around the pitch to try a shot at goal. Brett scurried behind the goals and grabbed his keeper, who seemed to be shivering violently in the goalmouth. Mally shot and the ball hit the top right-hand corner of the net. One-nil.

"What's up, Brett?" asked Mally's dad. "You look as if you've seen a ghost!"

"Nuffin'," growled Brett, rearranging his players. He was about to kick off, when he was unnerved by a strange noise from the garden. It was impossible to hear clearly from within the house, but it sounded very much like a crackly, metallic voice shouting instructions.

"What on earth was that?" asked Mally's dad, shooting from his armchair and dashing off to investigate. Mally followed closely behind, with Brett hanging back in the kitchen.

"Come here, quick!" called Mally's dad. "Mally, Brett, come *now*!"

Brett nervously popped his head around the back door and stepped onto the dark patio to see what was causing the commotion. At the bottom of the gloomy garden, in front of a demolished fence panel, he saw a vision that turned his blood to ice. A red, menacing-looking Dalek with two lights illuminating its domed head, scrutinized them with its solitary eye. Brett wanted to run for all he was worth, but his legs had other ideas.

"Brett Spittle, *you will be DESTROYED!*" screeched the unearthly, maniacal voice.

Brett began to bite his nails, four at a time.

"We have heard about you," it continued, it's eerie, mechanical cackle rising in pitch and distorting wildly. "You are a bully. You cause pain and suffering to the children at your earthling school, *so you must be EXTERMINATED!*"

"No, no leave me alone!" screamed Brett, terrified.

The Dalek's ray gun began to flash with red light.

"Brett Spittle, we have just implanted you with, erm, Space Bacteria as a warning to mend your ways. This will cause a chemical reaction in your body. The bacteria will wear off after two days, but if you continue to bully the others, we will return, *and seek you out.* I have hypnotized your fellow earthlings with my, erm, magic eye, so they will remember nothing of this. Brett Spittle – beware the power of the DALEKS. *You will be DESTROYED!*"

At this, the Dalek spun around, and exited stage-left through the flattened fence, into the darkness.

The effect on Brett was dramatic. Suddenly, after the earlier breakdown in communications, his legs once again decided to enter into a meaningful dialogue with his brain. He shot through the house and out of the front door like a prize greyhound after a rabbit, not even pausing to gather up his Subbuteo team. Mally and father strolled down the garden, laughing hysterically, and encountered a Dalek behind the fence, struggling to remove its own head.

"Absolutely brilliant!" grinned Mally, helping David out of Len's wonderful creation. "It went like a dream."

David picked up his megaphone and spoke into it.

"Brett has been *DESTROYED!*"

The party was joined by Mally's mother. "I almost felt sorry for him as he catapulted through our living room, heading for the front door," she chortled, "but from what Malcolm's told me about him, I shouldn't do. It serves him right for saying my mashed potato tasted funny. Mind you, I can't blame him. It did have twelve cloves of garlic grated into it!"

CHAPTER 11

Brett causes a stink

"How did the rehearsal go last night?" asked David's mother over breakfast.

"Oh, erm, good, thanks," mumbled David. "Mr Lewis thought dad's Dalek was incredible."

"Did he now?" asked Ruby. "Was that before or after your dad saw him with his mate, having a few pints in the Church Tavern?"

"Ah!"

"Ah indeed. Don't think that I'm being nosy, but exactly why did you get your dad to spend all weekend building a hardboard robot with flashing lights, and make me spend all day Monday undercoating it? We haven't got enough gloss left for the front door now, should it ever need touching up."

David felt it was time to come clean. He explained his complex and inventive plot to a dumbstruck parent and then cringed, awaiting the backlash. None came.

"I see," said Ruby, still reeling. "So that little swine has hit you, and you were too scared to tell me."

"He only hit me in the first place because I told you, and every time I tell you, he'll hit me some more, so I decided to get my own back another way."

"An expensive, time-consuming way, you mean?"

"Sorry, mom. Dad always says 'just hit them back', but it's not that simple. Some people aren't built for fighting. If I hit Brett back, he'd just pail me senseless. My way is better. He hasn't got a clue that Mally, Gary and me are behind it. He thinks the Daleks have injected him with space bacteria, and hopefully it'll make him think twice before he hits someone else."

Ruby had a very vivid imagination, and while David was rambling on, she was visualizing the whole bizarre scenario in her head, from the moment Doctor Hoon thought he spied an errant Dalek glide past his surgery, to the part where Brett skedaddled like a terrified greyhound. As a consequence of this, she suddenly embarked on one of her famed giggling fits, and David knew he wouldn't get any sense whatsoever out of her for at least ten minutes. Even after that, she was prone to wind herself up and start all over again without warning.

Eventually, she was able to force a sentence out without cracking up.

"And you think he believed it?" she spluttered, tears rolling down her cheeks.

"Definitely."

"But you'd have to be a bit stupid to think Doctor Who was real, surely?"

"Erm, y-yes, obviously." David turned the colour of a pillar-box. He moved on rapidly. "The newspaper did the trick, I think. Uncle Bill set the type and proofed a cover for me in his break. It was him that wrote the text underneath as well."

"And you did the voice? I'm surprised Brett couldn't tell right away."

"Ah! It was the megaphone that disguised it, you see. And I studied how they talked at Uncle Bill's house. They start normal, and then they always go higher at the end, and sound a bit crazy, like this; You will *be DESTROYED!*"

Ruby was reduced to hysterics again, so David left her to it. Besides, he had to get off to school.

* * *

David met up with Mally and Gary at first break for a debriefing session. Gary was beside himself with glee, due to a stunning performance against Crystal Palace the night before. Admittedly, Derek Batham had not exactly put up much of a fight, but even so, a score of thirty-seven – one was a remarkable result, considering that Gary had never played a match in his life till the week before. David and Mally were due their own first round matches at the weekend, and both doubted they'd survive. Mally had been drawn against Robert Glazier, and David was to play away against a very skilful lad called Nigel Genner – the only boy at the school who had ever beaten Robert Glazier.

All this was, of course, jolly interesting, and usually would have been the main topic of discussion over a luke-warm milk at playtime, but this was not any old day. Gary was desperate to hear what had happened to Brett, and Mally and

David were equally keen to impart the information. Unfortunately, the press conference had to be postponed, due to the close proximity of Brett himself, who'd decided to plonk himself on a low wall just feet away. Shaun, eager to have a word, ran over to join him, but as he got within a yard of the lad, he recoiled as if someone had hung a ten-week-old maggot-infested kipper under his nose.

"Flippin' heck!" he winced. "You stink alarming! What yer done, dropped into a sewer or what?"

Brett's hands formed into tight fists, but curiously, he seemed to make a conscious effort and unclenched them again.

"What do yer mean?"

"Can't yer smell it? You stink, I'm not kidding!"

"Are you having me on, 'cause if you are, I'll pail yer."

"Honest, no. It's unbearable. Trev, come here. Smell him."

Trev came over and took a sniff at close quarters. He gagged, and was almost sick. This did not go down well with Brett, whose fists were beginning to form again.

"I can't smell nuffin'," growled Brett.

"A fox can never smell his own cack," explained Shaun, helpfully.

Brett seemed to have become unusually sensitive about his body odour for a change, and stormed off, heading for the classrooms. This was odd. Ordinarily, he had to be dragged kicking and screaming into class after break. Now he appeared to be giving up his playtime in order to be alone with his thoughts, like some diminutive, pug-ugly eleven-year-old male version of Greta Garbo. This amused David and Mally no end. They waved him a fond farewell, and continued to fill Gary in on the night's events.

The bell sounded to herald the end of morning playtime and pupils returned to their classrooms. Mr Lewis asked if anyone had seen him in the newspaper, and a sea of hands rose in the air, giving the room the unfortunate appearance of a Hitler Youth rally.

"Sir, sir!" You looked proper silly," Megan cheerfully informed him. The rest of the class were more or less of the same opinion.

"Yes, thank you, Megan. Do you know, children, we still haven't had one single response to that article, which is most odd. I know old Jeremiah was a loner, but I thought *someone* would have owned one of his pieces of furniture, or at least known something about him. I'm beginning to think we collectively imagined the whole thing, and the tree never fell down in the first place. Mass hysteria they call it, apparently!"

Mr Lewis's far-fetched theory was interrupted by a rap on the door. Derek Batham entered, looking flushed. He had called on every classroom in the school, and could now empathize with Pheidippedes, the original Greek Marathon runner, coincidentally the subject of Mr Perriman's reading in assembly that very morning.

"Please sir, can everyone go to the hall right away please?" he gasped. "Mr Perriman wants a word with all the pupils, sir!"

Mr Lewis frowned. His lower lip extended. He scratched his chin in puzzlement. This mass exodus was virtually

126

unprecedented in his time at the school. Whatever had happened, it was serious. He called the class to order and sent them down to the hall, walking closely behind. One by one, other classroom doors opened, and more and more children followed suit, like a scene from The Pied Piper of Hamelin. The teachers glancing at each other in the hope that one of their number could provide additional information. None could.

The prefects shepherded the younger children into rows and instructed them to sit down cross-legged on the floor. Just behind them came the middle years, who sat on long form benches, and finally the senior pupils who sat on chairs. When every last child was in place, Mr Lewis called for order, and a hush fell over the hall. Mr Perriman strode across the stage with a face like thunder, and positioned himself behind his beautiful oak lectern, with the carved Staffordshire knot motif.

"I have called you all here for a very important reason," he began. His delivery, and for that matter, his looks, were reminiscent of Winston Churchill, a man he was known to greatly admire.

"Never, in the history of this school, have I had to do this before, and it fills me with sadness. I apologize, firstly, to my loyal staff, whose lessons I have interrupted. This, however, is a very serious matter. At first break, I left my office to use the lavatory. (Cue stray giggles, quickly extinguished by Mr Lewis.) While I was away from my room - and it must have been no more than two minutes – one of you entered my study and took a large amount of cash from the tin on my desk. This was the entire school's dinner money for the week, and now it has gone."

Brian Foley, a large, roly-poly lad from class 5C looked panic-stricken, fearing that he would not get fed. He was quietly reassured and told to calm down by Miss Hancox, the music teacher.

"I want whoever took this money to come forward, own up and be punished," continued Mr Perriman, gravely. "If you do this, nothing more will be said about it. If you don't, I may have to involve the police."

The hall was as silent as the grave. Children looked around at other children. At the back of the room, surrounded by empty seats, sat Brett Spittle, arms folded tightly. He stared at the stage, neither looking left or right, his hot little face looking fit to burst.

"I will return to my study now," concluded the Headmaster, "and await a visit from one of you. I am going to allow ten minutes for whoever did this to look to his or her conscience and do the right thing. A lot of parents who send their children to this school do not have much money, and we cannot afford to lose such a large amount ourselves either. Now, Mr Lewis, if you will be so kind as to lead the children out of the hall and back to their lessons. Thank you!"

Immediately, three hundred anxious voices erupted into a cacophony of noise. Brett Spittle slouched out of the hall, leaving a pungent block of air behind him, like some kind of malevolent, giant skunk.

Mr Lewis asked David and Mally, who were prefects, to guide the pupils back to their classroom and try to keep order for five minutes. As Deputy Head, he needed to pay a visit to the Headmaster in his lair and hear more. He tapped the head's door and was asked to enter. Inside, Sam Perriman was seated at his desk, fuming.

"Ah, hello Dai," he grunted. "Can you believe it? In all my years, this has never happened before. I admit, I should have locked the cash away, but I was gone for seconds, really. Whoever took this money must have been watching from the corridor, and chanced his or her luck."

"What's that blooming awful smell?" asked Mr Lewis. "Can you smell it?"

"I can, actually. I thought it was the drains blocked again, but it's not quite the same smell is it? It's an awful stench. Pungent is the word."

"You don't think something's died under your desk, do you?"

"Not unless I did, and nobody told me. Anyway, it's been five minutes already, and no-one has tapped on my door yet, except you of course, and I presume you didn't do it."

"Correct. So what now, presuming no-one owns up?"

"Reluctantly, I call the police. What else can I do?"

"Nothing, I suppose. Look, I have to return to my class, before they run riot. I'll see you at twelve-thirty and we can chat over dinner, that's if we can afford any."

Mr Lewis marched down the corridor and intercepted Brett Spittle as he sloped out of the boy's lavatories.

"Get back to class, Brett," snapped the teacher. "I'd like to know who gave you permission to…."

Mr Lewis sniffed the air. He sniffed again. "Come back here, boy, if you would," he shouted.

Brett walked slowly and reluctantly back to his form teacher.

"Right, get closer."

"Why?"

"Just come here, please. Goodness me, not *that* close! Good God! That's revolting! What on earth have you been rolling in?"

"Nuffin'."

Mr Lewis's brow was corrugated with deep thought.

"Turn out your pockets, Brett, please."

Brett did as he was told. They contained half a Woodbine cigarette and a packet of Bazooka Joe bubble gum. He flashed his teacher an evil look. If looks could kill, Mr Lewis would have been a mass of contusions, at the very least.

The astute young Welshman wasn't satisfied. "Let's take a look at the back pocket, lad."

"No!"

"Why not?"

"There's nuffin' in it, that's why not."

"So show me."

"No."

"Then I'll take a look myself."

He spun the boy around, wishing that he still had his father's World War Two gasmask, and immediately noticed a large mass within the back pocket.

"Either this is padding in readiness for the caning you suspect you might be about to get – a great wad of 'Izal Medicated' toilet paper is it? – or else it's the money itself."

He reached inside the pocket and pulled out a large bundle of cash.

"I'm afraid you and I have to see the headmaster, young Brett," said Mr Lewis sternly. He grabbed the boy by the collar and frog-marched him in the direction of Mr Perriman's study. As they approached, Brett became more and more agitated, and landed a kick on Mr Lewis's shin in protest.

Mr Lewis grimaced in pain, and manhandled the little thug into the office without bothering to knock, much to Mr Perriman's surprise.

"Our thief, Mr Perriman. Lord knows what he's been doing, but there's a foul smell coming from every pore in his body. It's the same smell that we experienced in your office. I searched him, and the money was in his back pocket. I don't think we need any more proof, do you, sir?"

"I've had the windows open, and you can *still* smell it," growled the head teacher. "What on earth have you done to yourself, boy?"

Brett went white and began to tremble. "It's space bacteria. A Dalek injected me with it!"

"Don't be ridiculous!" snapped Mr Perriman. "This is no time for silly remarks. You are in big trouble, Brett. You've been caught red-handed. Now I intend to give you six strokes of the cane, and we'll hear no more about it. Is that understood?"

131

"You ain't caning me!" screamed Brett.

"Well, I can see your parents about this and call the police, if you prefer, young man," replied Mr Perriman, through gritted teeth. "Now what is it to be?"

Brett shook himself free of Mr Lewis's grasp and bolted out of the room. He rocketed down the main corridor and out of the front doors, heading for the banks behind the school and showing a similar turn of speed to that he showed when the Dulux Dalek threatened to exterminate him.

* * *

It was during afternoon playtime that Mr and Mrs Spittle arrived, with Master Spittle in tow. David was on playground duty with Mally and Gary, standing watch on the entrance to the main corridor, when they confronted him. It was the prefect's job to make sure no-one entered the building without permission during break, and security had been stepped up to red alert following the theft.

"Move out of the way," snarled Mrs Spittle, "we've come to see your blasted headmaster."

"Do you have an appointment?" asked David, following his script to the letter.

"No, we bloody don't, now shift!" she raged.

"I'm not allowed to let anyone in unless they have an appointment," repeated David, terrified but determined to hold his ground.

"H-h-he's right, actually," explained Mally, cowering behind his friend.

Mrs Spittle roughly manhandled the three boys out of her way and rampaged through the corridor in search of a fight. David and Mally ran after them with Gary bringing up the rear, trying to head them off at the pass and warn their teacher. Mr Lewis, who was walking down the corridor from the staff room, met the full force of Hurricane Spittle.

"Nobody canes my Brett," she screamed. "He didn't steal no money. He's sworn it weren't him, and I believe my lad."

Mr Perriman joined the group, having heard the commotion from his study. He asked Mrs Spittle to keep her voice down while children were around and begged Brett's angry parents to accompany him to the privacy of his room.

"Cane Brett, and I'll break every bone in your body," threatened Mr Spittle, who, until now, had said nothing.

"Excuse me," interjected Mr Lewis, chivalrously stepping in front of his ageing head teacher. "I caught your boy red-handed with over a hundred pounds in his trousers. We offered him a punishment that would prevent him from having a serious criminal record at the age of eleven. If you would prefer that we called the police, then so be it. As to breaking every bone in Mr Perriman's body, the contest is hardly a fair one, wouldn't you say? My boss here is sixty-two and you are around twenty-eight. You're far nearer my age than his. Now, we can handle this in a dignified fashion, and accept that the boy must take his punishment, or else I can take you out to the playing field and see what happens. Before we do that though, I must warn you that I boxed for Wales, and was Henry Cooper's sparring partner for two years before I entered the teaching profession. Now which is it to be, Mr Spittle?"

"Take him outside and give him a good hiding," suggested Mrs Spittle. "He's probably making it up about boxing for Wales anyway!"

"That's for you to find out, boyo!" smiled Mr Lewis.

"Let's talk this over," suggested Mr Spittle, exercising a rare moment of caution.

"Pail him, dad!" suggested Brett.

"Why don't you?" invited Mr Lewis, drawing himself up to his full height of six-foot-one.

"Look, let's all calm down," said Mr Spittle.

"*We* already are," Mr Lewis reminded him. "It's you that burst in here threatening violence. Now we intend to cane your son and say no more about it. Do you agree, or shall we phone the police? It's a simple choice."

"Nobody lays a hand on my Brett," hissed Mrs Spittle.

"Cane him," sighed Mr Spittle.

"What?" shrieked Brett. "Dad? You said you'd sort it out."

"I have done," groaned his crestfallen father. "Cane him, and then forget about it, is that a deal?"

"Yes, unless of course he does this again," chipped in Mr Perriman.

Mrs Spittle glared at her husband, but such was the menacing look he reciprocated with that she remained silent. Brett, on the other hand, was panicking more than somewhat.

"I did it because I hated everybody calling me smelly," he blurted out, his face crimson with frustration and anger. "Nobody would sit by me or talk to me, and they kept holding their noses and asking me if I'd pooed my pants or eaten a dead rat. It's not my fault. A Dalek injected me with space bacteria, and it's made me stink. Mally Lobes won't remember though, 'cause he was hypnotized. I was trying to be good all day, like the Dalek said I had to, but everybody kept calling me names."

Mr Lewis turned to Mr Perriman, who stared blankly back at him. Neither had a ready comment to make. Brett's outburst seemed to take them into deep and uncharted waters again.

"Stop talking garbage, you little cretin," snapped Mrs Spittle, cuffing him with force around the head.

The three prefects had witnessed the entire confrontation in silence until now, and it was a shock to all when Gary suddenly spoke.

"You've been calling me horrible, nasty names every day since I've been here," he said with quiet dignity, his bottom lip trembling. "Names that made me cry myself to sleep every night. How do *you* like it?"

"Okay lads," said Mr Lewis, "run along to your classrooms now please."

"Your stink will go away, but my leg won't. Mr Perriman told us about the Ten Commandments in assembly. Do as you would be done by. If you're nice to other people, they'll be nice to you, Brett."

"Don't get yourself upset, Gary," said Mr Lewis gently. "Off to your classrooms, lads, please."

"Please don't cane him, sir. Please!" begged Gary, somewhat surprisingly. "Give him another chance. Turn the other cheek, you always say. Forgiveness is a virtue. You tell us that in assembly."

For someone who professed to be an atheist, Gary knew his bible. Brett just looked uncomfortable and embarrassed.

"That's quite enough," barked the headmaster. "Off you trot. Mr and Mrs Spittle, I'll see you privately in my study."

Mr Perriman asked the Spittle family and Mr Lewis to be seated. He cleared his throat, as if to deliver a major speech to war-torn Europe via an old BBC radio microphone.

"Mr and Mrs Spittle, I have been thinking this through as we stood in the corridor, and I have made a decision. I beg you to give this serious thought. That little boy with polio, Gary Leyton, has a habit of pricking consciences. He has reminded me that we are a Christian school. It's no good my preaching to them in assembly if I then ignore my own lessons in full view of the pupils. That said, please don't make the mistake of thinking I am a pushover. Your son, Brett here, has been a major problem at this school. I will not mince my words, Mrs Spittle. As parents, both of you have been in denial, refusing to accept that he could do any wrong. This must stop. He has ransacked the place, caused more fights than I can count and bullied, yes bullied, Mrs Spittle, a good many children who were too terrified to tell on him. I am no fool, and I know what goes on in the playground. I have my spies."

"But…"

"Be quiet and listen, Mrs Spittle. Then you may speak. I am not going to cane your boy, though it is perfectly within my rights so to do. I will give him one last chance to reform, or he can look forward to a life of borstal and eventually jail, as he grows up and his crimes get worse. Do you really want this for your son, or will you help us? Brett's six strokes of the cane are to be kept on the books, so to speak, and if he is guilty of one more misdemeanour, he will get twelve, and I will expel him. Is that understood? One more cruel, nasty name called, one more window broken, one more child punched until he cries, one more stray cat kicked, and he is for the high jump. Now, for my part, I'm going to involve young Brett in school life. I admit, we have steered clear of him because he is such trouble. From now on, I'll encourage whatever talents he has. If he likes fighting, then maybe we'll teach him boxing. We'll channel his aggression into cross-country running or whatever he fancies. We'll all try harder – we, the teachers, you the parents, and mostly Brett Spittle - you. Remember, whatever you do has a big impact on others. Do as you would be done by. You were terrified that I was going to cane you, weren't you? I saw the fear in your face. Well that is how your victims feel when you approach them. Now go away and think about that deeply."

The Spittles stood up and shuffled to the door, muttering half-hearted apologies under their breath. Mr Lewis, in particular, had expected more of a cat-fight, but it had been a very lacklustre performance by their standards. They had taken a substantial kicking and they didn't like it, but somewhere, deep down inside all three of them, they knew the Headmaster was right.

He closed the door behind them and breathed a huge sigh of relief.

"Well Sam, that was brilliant, I must say," said Mr Lewis. "Statesmanlike I'd call it, and they certainly got the point.

Strong, yet forgiving. We ought to carve that motto under the Staffordshire Knot on your lectern!"

"Thank you, Dai. Call me naïve, but somehow, I feel we may have turned a corner with the Spittles. We can but live in hope. Incidentally, you're a dark horse, old son. I had no inkling that you'd actually boxed for Wales and sparred with our Henry."

"Ah, well that's probably because it was a pack of lies, Sam - a complete pack of lies. I've never hit anyone in anger in my whole life. I was scared stiff, my friend!"

CHAPTER 12

Miracles do happen

Mr Lewis burst into the staffroom like a Texan Marshall entering a frontier saloon bar. Had there been a honky-tonk pianist playing, he would have stopped and hidden behind his piano. The teachers, who had previously been enjoying their chocolate biscuits and coffee, all ceased chewing and turned to their deputy leader, hanging on his every word.

"You will *never* guess what I have just witnessed," he began, his eyes like saucers.

"Alien invasion?" suggested Mrs Hancox.

"Nothing so prosaic," he countered.

"School milk at the perfect temperature?" asked Mr Perriman.

"No, Head. Come on – I didn't say it was a miracle. Mind you, it's pretty damned close, I have to admit. I have just seen, with my own eyes, Brett Spittle ask Gary Leyton to show him how to play chess."

"Excuse my pedantic nature," interrupted Mr Evans, who had an English degree, "but I think you meant 'heard with my own ears', not 'seen with my own eyes', Dai boy."

"Look, whatever! The point is, well, it's amazing isn't it?"

"It certainly is," admitted Mr Perriman, chewing on a reflective biscuit."

"And I'm also pleased to announce that the unearthly smell has more or less disappeared too, thank God!"

"What on earth *was* that?" asked Mr Perriman. "It reminded me of garlic, but fifty times more pungent. When I was in the army, we had this Italian chap who switched sides and came to work for us on Salisbury Plain. A top intelligence bod he was, but he used to pong of garlic every morning, thanks to all the foreign muck he used to eat. This smelled just like that, but amplified to the power of fifty. Lord knows what Mrs Spittle's feeding her boy, but if she ever invites us round for tea, which frankly is highly unlikely, we need to think of an excuse in advance."

"And what about the gibberish he was spouting? I think he was delirious."

"You're right! That's one of the reasons I didn't cane the little beggar, to be honest. He seemed so fearful of what was coming, he was speaking in tongues. The smell, apparently, was caused by space bacteria, but Malcolm Stevens was hypnotized, so he couldn't remember anything about it."

The staffroom roared with laughter. Mr Simmons choked on his biscuit.

"Well, I couldn't do it to the lad after that. Fear makes people do strange things, and with Brett, it brought on a form

140

of delirium. Imagine if I'd gone ahead and striped his backside, and he'd become totally psychotic. I couldn't live with myself."

"Well, hopefully, we've turned a corner with the boy," concluded Mr Lewis. "It's early days of course, but you never know."

"Agreed," smiled Mr Perriman. "If we've made a difference to that lad's life, it's all been worthwhile, I say."

Mr Lewis was warming to his theme now.

"It dawned on me after that scene yesterday, that maybe we should be doing more to encourage the ones we tend to ignore. We're only human, after all, and it's always easier to spend time with kids who are willing to learn. I also think we don't involve them enough in school decisions. We always choose what the school play's going to be about without asking them. We ignore their little fads and playground games. If we involved them, they'd automatically be more enthused wouldn't they?"

"Such as?"

"Well, let them vote on what the school play's going to be about, for starters, and maybe let them actually write it. We'd have to steer them of course, but the trick is to make them *think* they've created it all by themselves. They're all mad about Subbuteo at the moment. I know it's a fad, and next year it'll be something else, but why not let them hold their matches at school during dinner times, and offer them a little trophy. One of us could volunteer to referee, and save them squabbling and falling out."

"Brilliant idea!" said Mr Evans, patting his colleague on the back. "Good of you to give up your lunchtimes to ref their games."

"Oh, I wouldn't mind," replied Mr Lewis. "I really wouldn't."

"Well, I'm certainly not against it in principle," agreed Mr Perriman. "We must all remember that we are ancient and boring to these kids – especially me. Hopefully, something like this would get them on our side. If you want to take it on board, you go ahead."

* * *

It was time to remove David's stitches, and he was dreading it. Due to a ten o'clock appointment with Doctor Hoon, he'd not been to school that morning, and consequently missed the near miracle that was unfolding in the library. Not only had Brett Spittle asked Gary to show him the rudiments of chess, he'd refrained from punching the lad when he lost his queen after five moves. Brett had also thanked Gary for helping to spare him a caning, for which he was extremely grateful, and offered his chess partner a grubby Bazooka Joe from the depths of his pocket – an offer that was politely refused. After all, his gammy leg had been caused by a diseased Polo mint - according to Mally at any rate - and there was no way he was risking his good leg by ingesting a suspect bubble gum.

Undaunted by this rebuttal, Brett continued trying to spread sweetness and light. He even offered Gary protection in the playground, so that, if anyone dared call him Spaz again, Brett would personally beat them up. Again, this was politely but firmly refused. Undoubtedly, Brett was changing, but there was still along way to go. One couldn't expect a complete transformation from devil to angel overnight.

David was invited into the surgery and asked to sit down on the edge of a couch. Doctor Hoon, preliminary niceties concluded, examined the wound and declared his handiwork a success.

"You'll be left with a nasty red scar there, I'm afraid, and the skin will always look like tissue paper, but it has healed nicely. Did you ever go back down the side of the garage and find the missing bit?"

"Change the subject, please!" insisted Ruby, clutching the edge of the doctor's table.

"Sorry, Mrs Day. I forgot you were a bit squeamish. "Now this will sting a bit, but nothing awful. Mrs Day, go and sit in the waiting room."

The doctor removed the stitches as gently as he could. David looked away and winced a few times, but within seconds it was all over, and his faint-hearted mother was invited back.

"He's a brave lad, Mrs Day," said the doctor. "All done! Incidentally, how's that neighbour of yours getting on with his little finger? Does it still work?"

"Yes," replied David. "It looks a bit strange – a bit like its owner really - but it does work. Shouldn't they have sewn it back so that the nail was on the same side as the other four though?"

"You *are* joking!" groaned the good doctor. "They never sewed it on backwards?"

David was hopeless at keeping a straight face.

"Oh yes, you are joking, you little devil. You had me going for a second then. And how's the lad with polio getting on? He seemed like a nice little fellow."

"He is, he's my equal best friend," smiled David.

"The reason I ask is that I've just been reading the Lancet, which is a magazine for us doctors, and there's a lot of pioneering work going on in America to do with polio-affected limbs. They're working on leg-stretching and strengthening techniques that sound as if they'd help your Gary a lot. Trouble is, everything comes at a price, unfortunately. You might like to keep the article and show it to his parents, next time you see them."

David thanked the doctor and passed on the article to his mother for safekeeping. The pair stood up to leave, when the good doctor decided to have a bit of fun at David's expense.

"Oh, one last thing. Do you still believe that Doctor Who is real, and that Daleks are roaming Brierley Bank?"

David flushed red. "No, of course not. Do you?"

* * *

David arrived back at school in time for double English, one of his favourite subjects. Mr Lewis, always enthusiastic, was even more so for some reason.

"Children," he began, "the school play is upon us again. I've had a word with Mr Perriman, and he agrees that this year, we will allow you to choose the theme of the play.

Once this is agreed by a vote, you will all be asked to help write the script or act in it. Those who don't fancy that will operate the curtains, lights and so on. Let's have some hands up for ideas. You Barry!"

"Sir, sir! Spaceships, sir!"

"Very interesting, Barry. Anyone else?"

"Sir, puppies, sir!"

"Yes, erm, good suggestion, Celia? Paul?"

"Sir, Doctor Who, sir!"

"Ah, Doctor Who. That's very popular at the moment, I hear. Anyone else for spaceships and Doctor Who?"

A sea of hands expressed their support.

"Very well. Time travel, Doctor Who, spaceships. We can use all that."

"What about puppies?"

"Yes, Celia, we'll get some puppies in there somewhere, I'm sure. Now, those who fancy themselves as scriptwriters, see me after class and we'll try to come up with a decent plot. Maybe the Daleks have captured some, erm, puppies and the Doctor has to get them back. Anyway, we'll see, shall we?"

The children received this news with much enthusiasm, and were uncontrollable for at least five minutes. Eventually, when order was restored, Mr Lewis introduced the next item on his agenda.

"Right, silence, please. I'm afraid that this is mainly for the boys, but we'll try and organize something equally good for the girls as soon as possible. I'm aware that most of you are involved with this here Subbuteo league. Mr Perriman and I have agreed that we could play matches in the school hall at lunchtimes and maybe after lessons. I'd volunteer to keep order and referee the games to avoid rows, and we will provide you with a little engraved trophy for the league winner each year. How's that?"

To say the response was rapturous was an understatement. If the bottom fell out of the teaching market, Mr Lewis could have made an impression as a politician. He certainly knew how to butter up a crowd.

"We already have a trophy for the F.A. Cup, sir," piped up David. "You gave it to me, remember?"

"Yes. Did your dad ever succeed in straightening it?"

"Yes, sir. It's still a bit wonky, but much much better."

"Okay, fair enough. We'll purchase a new trophy for the league then. How's that?" The teacher flung an arm around his pupil's shoulder, and seemed desirous of a quiet word. "Now, while I've got you, young David, I need to ask a favour. If I were to grease your talented father's palm with twenty quid, do you think he'd build us a Dalek for our school play, by any chance?"

David smiled one of his mysterious smiles. "I'm sure of it, actually. Yes, absolutely, sir!"

That lunchtime, Robert Glazier handed over his fixtures list to Mr Lewis, who pinned a large chart on the staffroom notice-board. From that moment on, the games would be played at school with proper records kept and proper rules adhered to. No longer would Ian Garrington be allowed to call 'Blocks!' whenever he was in danger of losing. No more would players be able to kneel on their opponent's teams, either by accident or design. A new pitch was to be purchased and mounted onto the table-tennis table, and competitors would stand up to play. A mini-stadium of thirty seats would be constructed around the pitch, to create a bit of atmosphere. Subbuteo the spectator sport had arrived.

Over the course of the next week, league games were arranged virtually every day, and the F.A. Cup had progressed to the semi-final stage. Robert Glazier, the favourite, was still in the running, as were Trevor Jones and Ian Garrington. Less predictable, however, was the fourth semi-finalist, Gary Leyton. When most young boys were practising keeping a football up in the air using the head, feet and knees during playtime, Gary applied the same dedication to Subbuteo. He would flick little players around for hours and hours, perfecting his spin and dribbling manoeuvres. He would shoot balls at the tiny plastic nets time and time again, until he could score with his eyes closed. His legs may well have been a bit wonky, as he was first to admit, but he had fingers like Stanley Matthews.

The semi-finals were played to a capacity dinnertime crowd, some of whom had forsaken their fish fingers to attend. Gary had drawn Ian Garrington, and was quietly and clinically annihilating the poor little chubby creature. When the final whistle put him out of his misery, the score was twenty-three – two. It was a popular win, largely due to a lot of personal bitterness from previous opponents of Garrington, who had fallen foul of his quick temper and ad-hoc rules.

Gary, still flushed with success, and seemingly never tired of playing the game, had arranged a friendly at David's house that evening. Rightly assessing sixty-five - ten as an unassailable lead, Manchester City conceded.

"You didn't play as badly as the score-line suggests," said Gary magnanimously, as they packed their teams away. "Thanks for the game anyway. I needed to get a bit of extra practice in, because it's final day tomorrow, and I'm against Glazier."

"Should be a great match," replied David. "It's a sell-out. Mr Lewis has had to put another row of seats in the stadium. It holds fifty now!"

"I just wish we could have found your granddad's head – you know, for the final," sighed Gary. "It's a shame that he's going to miss it."

"He'll be there in body and spirit!" laughed David, pleased with his little joke.

"Very good! It would have been nice to have a head on my number nine though. I keep thinking it's an omen. You know, unless we find it, I'll lose, sort of thing."

Ruby wandered into the living room and greeted Gary. She gave her son a stern look.

"Remember promising me something, a few weeks ago, young man?"

"What?"

"You said you'd clean Jennings's cage out, and I threatened that if you didn't, I'd give him away. Well, have you sniffed that cage lately? It stinks worse than Brett Spittle after twelve cloves of space bacteria."

"Sorry, mom. I'll do it now. Gary can help me, can't you Gary?"

Gary could hardly refuse such a generous offer, so he didn't. David staggered into the living room moments later with Len's deluxe rodent bachelor pad and laid it down onto the previous night's Express and Star. It was fair to say that the house didn't smell too sweet. David gingerly removed the sodden straw, filling the room with the pungent stench of ammonia. Jennings, glad to be away from his environment for a while, charged around the room with gay abandon, sniffing the skirting board. Gary changed the water and poured new seeds into the food troughs, leaving David the job of removing the poo. It was his hamster, after all.

Suddenly, David let out a triumphant yell. There, amongst the heady mixture of seeds and tiny black poos, was Granddad Reuben's head. He fished it out and buffed it up on a scrap of newspaper. Other than a passing resemblance to Al Jolson, grandpa had suffered no ill effects – if, of course, one ignored the fact that he had been decapitated.

Ruby ran into the room, thinking her son had accidentally burnt his backside on the three-bar gas fire, and was confronted by two delighted-looking children, one of whom was displaying a severed shrunken head in the palm of his hand.

"This is fate!" declared Gary. "I believe in that, I really do. Now the team's complete. Bring on tomorrow, I say; Aston Villa against Brierley Bank Celtic in the F.A. Cup Final, with your granddad Reuben leading out the team."

Jennings must have swallowed your granddad's head when you let him out last time," said Ruby. "Perhaps he thought it was a seed. It's exactly the same size!"

"So you're telling me," frowned Gary, "that my striker's head has been pooed out of a hamster's bottom?"

CHAPTER 13

Cup Final Day

It was Friday, which meant it was cup final day. Immediately after lunch – or dinner, as it was called by all right-minded Black Countrymen – most of the boys and a handful of girls headed for the hall, where the table was set up and ready. The atmosphere, it had to be said, was electric, and some children had even brought scarves. Peter Fisher of 6D had even managed to find a football rattle, but after several deeply irritating demonstrations of its ear-shattering volume, it was duly confiscated by Mr Lewis.

The two finalists entered the room amid wild cheering and were photographed shaking hands next to David's newly inherited battered trophy. Then, on Mr Lewis's whistle, Gary, having won the toss, limped around the table with his awkward, dipping gait to kick off. Possession was lost after a few nervous flicks, allowing Robert Glazier to pick up the ball and speedily manoeuvre it into Gary's penalty area. He flicked a powerful shot at goal, which catapulted off the crossbar and ended up in Margaret Parsons's lap. Once back in play, it was Robert again who seemed to be making the running. A beautiful long pass found his lone striker, who didn't make the same mistake twice. It was one – nil to Aston Villa. Unfazed by this early goal, Gary kicked off once more, and was soon in his opponent's goal area. A low, rifling shot was too quick for the Villa goalie, and it was one – all. The capacity crowd was ecstatic, and several of the more exuberant boys leapt from their seats cheering. The headmaster, who was accompanied by the Reverend McKenzie, entered the room just in time to see goal number three, a well-crafted effort by a Villa midfielder, which was all the more remarkable when one considered that the gentleman lacked both arms and half a leg.

From then on, the goals came fast and furious. The real Granddad Reuben had never scored a goal in his life, but his miniature namesake seemed intent on notching up a cricket score. Robert Glazier, himself no slouch on the green baize, could only watch as Gary expertly dribbled his way around the table, firing in shots from angles that even Joe Davis, the billiards legend would have found challenging.

By half-time, the Villa was no less than twelve goals down, and the players desperately needed an inspirational pep talk. Alas, there was no miniature manager on hand to cajole, coax and chide them, and the second half began as the first had ended, with a beautiful effort by granddad Reuben that had the keeper licked. The landslide seemed to be affecting Robert Glazier's nerve now, and he was making rash challenges and dubious tactical decisions. Even his rather bizarre nine-man defence with one very lone striker could not prevent the incredible onslaught, spearheaded once again by Brierley Bank's intrepid number nine. For a man of over sixty, his stamina touched on the superhuman, as he raced up and down the pitch, chivvying his men and leading by example. With only two minutes remaining until the final

152

whistle, the match was his for the taking, as long as he didn't lose his head.

Sensing that time was of the essence, Robert Glazier gamely fought back, scoring a quick three goals in succession, but it was too little too late. His final burst down the wing was interrupted by Mr Lewis's whistle, signalling that the inaugural Brierley Bank Junior School Subbuteo F.A. Cup was over, and Gary Leyton was its first ever winner. Touchingly, one of the first children to congratulate him, after David and Mally, was none other than Brett Spittle – a gesture that didn't go unnoticed by both Mr Perriman and Mr Lewis.

The two finalists shook hands once more, and Gary was asked to hold his wonky trophy aloft for more official photographs. History had been made, in two senses. Not only was this hopefully the start of a yearly competition, but also, a hopeless, non-league Sunday team full of invalids, captained by a granddad with a glued-on head had managed to beat Aston Villa thirty-seven – nine. Not only this, but with a manager-cum-coach who couldn't kick a ball straight to save his life, or run ten yards without falling over.

The Reverend McKenzie patted Gary on the back and strode over to have a word with Mr Lewis.

"I'm pleased I caught some of that," he smiled. "Very exciting it was too. I think I'd go to Villa Park more often if there were that many goals per game! That isn't why I'm here though, Mr Lewis. I've made some progress with our Mr Silversmith, so I thought I'd share it with you. You know I said that he didn't appear to exist, in terms of the parish records? Well, I've cracked it! The other day, a lady brought me a pile of old books for the jumble sale, and I was glancing through them when I found an inscription that made me sit up. The book was owned by a Mr Jeremiah Carpenter, and I thought to myself, 'That's a coincidence. I'm looking for a Jeremiah who *was* a carpenter! Well, the day after, I browsed through the parish records again, and found this Jeremiah Carpenter, and guess what? His dates are identical to Jeremiah Silversmith's. I thought this was too much of a coincidence, so I did some digging - not his grave, you understand. I located an article about Brierley Bank's stonemason at the time of Silversmith's death, a Mr Benjamin Batham, courtesy of your cup-winning pupil, Gary Leyton's father. He's in a local history society, you see, and this man Batham was a real character, by all accounts. He was an alcoholic – which Jeremiah actually refers to in his letter – and was infamous for getting the wording wrong on his gravestones, due to his inebriated state!"

"Well I never!" grinned Mr Lewis. "What a disgrace!"

"Exactly! So I re-examined the inscription on the grave, and voilà! Our man is actually Jeremiah Carpenter, the silversmith. It appears that no-one spotted the error, or if they did, couldn't be bothered to get it corrected. Jeremiah was, after all, a loner with no family, so I suppose nobody visited his grave or cared one way or the other."

"What a shame. He didn't even get his blooming name spelled correctly, after he'd paid good money for it."

"Yes, I agree. Quite a tragedy really. Anyway, the reason I dashed over to see you is this. After my breakthrough bit of detective work, I was able to trace Jeremiah Carpenter through the records, and with help from our history society friends I found out quite a bit about him. He was a very accomplished silversmith, and made such items as candelabras, crucifixes and so on, as opposed to the more mundane items like rings and jewellery that most silversmiths specialize in."

"Aha!" smiled Mr Lewis, "I can see where this is leading I think."

"Then I have to disappoint you, I'm afraid. The society has actually got copies of his old order books and invoices, which is fantastic. Our Mr Carpenter made a few items for my own church, and he always engraved a small J.C. underneath them."

"Very apt for a church, J.C."

"Yes, very funny! Our crucifix was actually made by him, and so are a few other bits and pieces, but I can't see how they could be hiding treasure of any kind, to be honest. The items themselves are very beautiful and made or solid silver, which is expensive of course, but we paid for those things at the time and we were just getting what we'd paid for. No, if I could explain; the reason I came here to see you was because he also made a few things for you."

"Me?" asked Mr Lewis, perplexed.

"The school, I mean. Mr Carpenter also made silver trophies. Our records show that he donated two such trophies to Brierley bank Junior School when it first opened, in eighteen-ninety-eight."

"Did he indeed?"

"Yes, he did. And did you notice that I said donated? Not sold, like the stuff we own at the church. That's the curious thing, don't you see? This miserly, penny-pinching fellow decides to donate two trophies to a school out of the goodness of his heart, months before he died."

"My God! Do you know which trophies they were? We have several." Mr Lewis was getting hot under the collar now.

"Yes, indeed. It says in the records that there were two large, identical silver cups – one for football and one for cricket, logically enough. Do you by any chance still have them?"

Mr Lewis groaned and buried his head in his hands.

"You're looking at one of them, vicar. It's that badly dented thing over there, being paraded around by Gary Leyton."

"Well, I suggest you get him to hand it back, pronto! Do you still have the other cup?"

"Yes, it's in our cabinet. I'll get a prefect to fetch it after I've looked at this one."

Mr Lewis strode over to Gary, who was still on cloud nine. The cup weighed around four tons, but he was determined to parade it around the hall above his head for his fans to see, until such time that Mr Perriman could arrange to lay on an open-topped bus.

"Erm, Gary," he smiled. "Well done, by the way. Could I, erm, possible take a look at your cup for a second?"

Gary handed it over, grateful for a rest. Mr Lewis scrutinized it inch by inch. Eventually, he located the small J.C. inscription, just under the lid. He shook the cup from side to side, and looked inside it. He scratched at it with a penknife, much to Gary's annoyance, and looked underneath its plinth. There was nothing obvious to be gleaned from his examination. The Reverend McKenzie appeared to be barking up the wrong tree. Then the penny dropped.

"This trophy is too heavy," he announced dramatically, the way Hercule Poirot liked to do when explaining evidence to house-guests in the oak-panelled library.

"You're telling me, sir!" agreed Gary.

"No, I mean, too heavy for what it appears to be made of. A silver cup, even of this size, shouldn't weigh this much."

The Reverend McKenzie scratched at his beard and glanced at the teacher, impressed by his grasp of elementary physics. Mr Lewis turned the cup over and examined the base. Usually, they were constructed of turned wood, or with less ancient trophies, black bakelite or plastic. The bottoms were always hollow; to lighten the weight, but this one had a solid feel to it. He peeled away the green baize which had been glued on to prevent the trophy scratching furniture, and was greeted by a false bottom. He employed his trusty penknife once more to prise away the thin wooden plate, and looked inside. What he saw took his breath away. He fell just short of emulating his hero, Howard Carter, by announcing to all those present that he could see wonderful things, but it was obvious to all those now looking on that he had discovered something very unusual indeed. Now he knew why the hollow wooden base felt so heavy.

It contained a circular block of solid gold.

"Oh my goodness!" whispered the dumbstruck teacher. "This must be worth an absolute fortune nowadays."

"If it is gold, it will be," agreed the vicar, who'd gone weak at the knees. And we haven't examined the other cup yet!"

Mr Perriman was dispatched to collect the Football cup, and arrived, puffing and panting with it minutes later. It too had a baize bottom, and a wooden plate beneath. Mr Lewis, his hand shaking and his brow sweating, feverishly removed the plate and let fly with a choice expletive that ordinarily would have earned him a severe reprimand from his head teacher. On this occasion, none came, largely due to the fact that Mr Perriman had simultaneously let fly with one of his own, and a juicier one at that.

The second cup's contents were identical to the first.

"We are rich!" said Mr Lewis, in a state of shock.

"You would be if it were your cup, sir!" David reminded them politely.

* * *

"Let me try to understand," groaned Mr Perriman. "You *gave* young David our cricket cup for his football competition?"

"Er, yes," admitted an embarrassed Mr Lewis, "but in fairness, Headmaster, it was flatter than a dead hedgehog when I gave it to him. Sir wouldn't have wanted to keep it, would he, David?"

"No, sir."

"I might have done, had I known it was full of gold bullion, Dai."

"Ah, well hindsight is a wonderful thing, Headmaster."

"Can't David keep the cup and just hand back the gold ingot?" asked the vicar, optimistically.

"No," said David. "It's not as simple as that, sir. You see, I had the trophy bashed into shape again by my dad, and then I donated it to the Subbuteo competition, so that the winner got to keep it. So now Gary owns it, sir. If it was still mine, I'd give it back, but it's not mine anymore."

"What if we ask Gary to give it back?" suggested the vicar, who was not known for letting things go, once he'd got his teeth into them.

"Erm, Gary doesn't want to, do you Gary?" asked David.

"I don't mind..." began Gary. His sentence was curtailed by a sharp kick to his good leg.

"Gary doesn't want to, sir."

David produced a grubby piece of paper from his trouser pocket. He flashed it at Mr Lewis, Mr Perriman and the vicar, before continuing.

"This is an article from the Lancet, sir. American doctors are doing pioneering work, it says, to correct the legs of children affected by poliomyelitis – that's polio for short - and I want Gary to keep the gold, so that he can have his wonky leg done, sir."

"I didn't know you subscribed to the Lancet, David," said Mr Lewis, amazed. "I've always figured you to be an arts man through and through."

"No, it wasn't my magazine, sir," David explained earnestly, "I just have the Eagle, the Beezer, The Beano and the Dandy. Doctor Hoon cut it out for me, and asked me to show it to Gary, but I've only just got round to it. The trouble is, Doctor Hoon said it cost a lot of money to send someone to America, and I know Gary's mom and dad haven't got too much, so when I just heard you talking about the gold, I realized that Jeremiah had finally done something good with his money."

Gary stared at his friend with a mixture of awe, admiration and not a little love.

"That's if Gary *wants* to have his wonky leg mended, of course," added David, blushing.

"I do, more than just about anything," blurted Gary, "but will a little lump of gold like that be enough to pay for a trip to America?"

"I'm no expert, but judging by the weight of it, I reckon it would go a long way to buying you your own plane!" estimated Mr Lewis.

Mr Perriman put his arm around David's shoulders.

"What a remarkable boy you are!" he smiled. "And you are absolutely right. Poor old Jeremiah has finally done something worthwhile after a lifetime of misery, and he obviously intended children to benefit. It's just a shame he couldn't be here to see what he's done. I think it only fair that Gary here keeps his trophy. We have the other one, after all, and that's worth a small fortune too. It doesn't pay to be greedy. Do you remember the story I told you in assembly about King Midas? Keep your wonky cup with our blessing, Gary, and we'll share the proceeds from ours with the vicar here. After all, it did all begin in his churchyard."

The Reverend McKenzie seemed suitably buoyed by this gesture. Throughout the proceedings, he had looked a little restless - like a vicar who had gambled a couple of quid on a three horse race and watched his nag fall at the last hurdle - and this latest conciliatory offer had raised his spirits no end.

David too, was experiencing mixed emotions. His altruistic gesture had made him feel inordinately proud of himself, but he was dreading having to explain to his parents why he'd just given a solid block of pure gold to his best friend, especially after the microscope incident. He chewed over the scenario in his mind, and decided that the best policy was to get the bad news over with first, and then, just as his long-suffering father was reaching for the lump hammer, tell him that Mr Lewis had offered him twenty quid for his Dalek.

CHAPTER 14

Friends Reunited

Summer 2007

An overwhelming feeling of nostalgia engulfed David, the second he stepped into the school hall. Everything was just as he remembered it, over forty years ago. He stopped to put on his spectacles, the better to identify any old boys, and immediately noticed the framed John Everett Millais print depicting an old seafarer pointing to the ocean and recalling adventures from his youth to two enthralled young boys. It was somehow heartening to see that whoever was running the old place nowadays had spent absolutely nothing on décor. David could almost smell the school dinners, which was hardly surprising, as the last one had only been served some seven hours previously. He could also hear, thanks to his vivid imagination, the recorder group rehearsing for the end-of-term concert, and the ghost of Mr Perriman addressing the assembly, stood behind his impressive oak lectern.

Oblivious almost to the group of fifty-somethings huddled around the drinks table at the far end of the room, David relived the cold, bleak day over twenty years previously, when he and five other ex-pupils had struggled into Brierley Bank Church under the weight of the headmaster's oak coffin, with the Staffordshire Knot carved onto the lid.

David glanced around at the climbing ropes and shuddered. How he hated those things. He could never get more than half-way up before sliding back to earth, exhausted, whilst other lads could scamper to the top effortlessly. He could never do forward rolls either, and whenever it was time to somersault over the vaulting horse, he would feel sick to the pit of his stomach. He looked down at the uneven parquetry floor tiles, where he'd sat cross-legged through a thousand boring assemblies, getting cramp. Where had all those years gone? In spirit he was still a child, but in body he was a fifty-two-year–old man with a receding hairline and reading glasses.

A grey-haired gentleman at the refreshments table turned to face him, and called out his name. He strode over, beaming from ear to ear. David knew that characteristic gait even before he knew the face, but now, thankfully, it was a shadow of its former self.

"Gary!" David exclaimed, striding over to meet his old friend halfway. "You haven't changed a bit. Well, maybe a bit – you've gone grey, but it's hair, I always say, so you should be grateful."

"And yours fell out!" grinned Gary.

"It did?" asked David, looking worried. He felt around on the top of his head in mock-desperation. "Jeez! I had no idea until you just informed me!"

The two men hugged each other warmly. It was the first time they had met for over thirty years.

"And what happened to your gammy leg? You just skipped across here like a spring chicken."

"Ah, well it's still there, as you well know, you flatterer, but thanks to you, it's a million percent better."

"Yes it certainly is! I was half expecting a postcard from you when I was in the first year at Tipperton Grammar, informing me that after nine months in California, you and your family had decided to stay."

"Well, it *was* wonderful, apart from the horrible physiotherapy and the operations, I must admit. Can you imagine how it opened my eyes - an eleven-year-old working class lad who'd only ever been as far as my mate's caravan in Tenbury Wells, suddenly swanning around in America? Mom and dad missed the Black Country though, the Banks's Mild, the pork scratchings and the speedway. I guess the lure of Brierley Bank was too strong for me too."

"Really?"

"No! Are you kidding? I'd have stayed there forever, but they were more settled here, so of course, I had to return with them. It changed my life though, that little lump of precious metal, and do you remember when you quietly but firmly informed the head that it was ours, not his? I still can't believe you had the cheek to do that at your tender age!"

"Yes, and I haven't changed much either. I'm still getting myself into all sorts of trouble with this impulsive nature of mine," admitted David.

"The thing is," Gary continued, "I felt very guilty too, because I'd been given all that money and the school had done well, but you and Mally got nothing at all out of it."

"Au contraire, mon ami," smiled David, "we got the *most* out of it, don't you see? To give is better than to receive, and all that malarkey. It might sound corny, but it's absolutely true. And besides, what about all those fabulous presents you sent both of us from America. It was like Christmas in our houses when they arrived."

"That's because it *was* Christmas, you buffoon!"

"Oh yeah! You're right. Anyhow, let's hear no more about your guilt. Just thank the Lord you had two of the best mates a lad ever had. Now shut up about it." David pretended to draw a zip across his lips, to further emphasize his point. "Right," he continued, "is anyone here that I'd know, other than you, of course? I haven't seen any of this lot for ages. I doubt I'd recognize most of them now. You see, I've retained my youthful, handsome looks, but I bet they all look ancient. It's a funny thing about reunions. Some folks seem to have been preserved in aspic, and others look old enough to be your granddad."

"Mr Lewis is here," replied Gary. "I was hoping he was still with us. He's brilliant for his age too. He must be eighty if he's a day, and he's come all the way from Cardiff."

"Oh, I'm so pleased to hear that. I'm dying to se him again, but it always worries me, meeting up with old teachers. They still talk to you as if you were eleven, and I find it really difficult to call them by their first names."

"Do you still have your parents?" asked Gary.

"Just my mom. Dad died of emphysema seven years ago, and broke my heart in the process. Do you know, I still get upset about him even now, when I'm driving home from a job far too late at night and listening to something melancholy like Joni Mitchell, or especially when I've got myself into a bit of a state over things. How about you?"

"Both alive, touch wood, but not in the best of health. Been on the guided tour yet?"

"No, just arrived. Is it all too sentimental for words?"

"Just a bit! I've just been to see the new art block that the football trophy helped pay for. I call it new, and it's probably forty years old now."

"I still find it incredible that a lump of metal could have helped finance that."

"And another lump financed this, thanks to you," grinned Gary, tapping his leg.

"Don't start thanking me again, Gary, for God's sake! You always thanked folks too much when you were a kid as well! I was just pleased to hear that the trip had been worthwhile for you. Besides, I wouldn't have missed it for the world; explaining to my parents what I'd done. 'Mom, dad, guess what? I've been given a solid gold ingot, but I let Gary keep it!' Once they understood why I'd done it, they were fine though. Dad just went down to his shed and filed a piece of wood to shreds, and he was okay after that. I think it was his way of releasing tension without inflicting physical violence on a minor."

David and Gary walked over to the trestle table, where Mr Lewis was standing talking to a man of around fifty with a dog-collar and a beard.

"Sorry to interrupt," said David. "Mr Lewis, David Day!"

The sprightly old gentleman turned round and beamed at his ex-pupil. "Well I never! How are you? Still drawing dinosaurs?"

This was a perfect example of what David had spoken to Gary about earlier. These teachers could never understand that their little pupils actually grew up and became men and women.

"Erm, yes I am, actually," admitted David sheepishly. "I've just painted some for the British Museum. Trust you to ask that. I haven't drawn a blooming dinosaur for forty years, since I was in your classroom, trying to show *you* how to draw one, and last week I was asked to paint a Tyrannosaurus and a Triceratops for a poster to promote the museum's new dinosaur automatons exhibition."

The man in the dog collar coughed a polite cough.

"David, can I introduce myself? I'm the new vicar of Brierley Bank. I bet you don't remember me."

"No, I'm sorry, it's probably the beard. Not many of us had them at eleven. Were you in my class?"

"I was. I'm Brett Spittle."

David nearly choked on his mini sausage roll. He took a fortifying gulp of Shiraz, but this seemed to make matters worse. Gary slapped him on the back, sending a tiny chunk of soggy food onto the parquet floor.

"Sorry!" said David, deeply embarrassed. "That was a shock. Brett Spittle. I never figured you as a man of the cloth!"

"No, I suppose you wouldn't, after suffering me at school."

"So when did you realize that the church was calling you?"

"Not until I was in my late teens, but something strange happened to me at this very school that changed my life. I'm not exaggerating when I refer to it as a deeply moving, spiritual experience. I'd been a little tearaway and a nasty piece of work – I know that, so you don't have to be polite and deny it. I'd rather not go into what actually happened, but let's say I turned a corner as a result of this, erm, happening. Well, not immediately after it, I admit. I got into trouble one last time, as you well know, when I stole the dinner money and I was facing a caning. Gary here begged the Head not to cane me – to give me one last chance. You see, Gary, I've never forgotten it. You probably don't realize this, but you, in conjunction with this, erm, experience I've just mentioned, helped change my life. I took that chance, and never looked back. I enrolled into a boxing club, which Mr Lewis kindly arranged for me, and I channelled my energies in that way, instead of bullying boys in the playground. I met lots of other young lads there who needed saving from a life of crime, so I sort of took it upon myself to help them find their way, and one thing led to another. Mr Lewis here used to box for Wales, you see, and I looked up to him as a bit of a hero."

"Yes, I vaguely remember you said you'd boxed for Wales," said David.

Mr Lewis took a very long sip of his red wine and tried to nod modestly at the same time, two actions that, ideally, should have been carried out separately. He was rewarded for his efforts by a long red stain down his cream trousers. In a desperate attempt to change the topic, he addressed Gary.

"And what happened to you after Brierley Bank Juniors, Master Leyton?"

"Oh, I became an accountant. I'm senior partner at Giles, Howarth and Nibblock now, and I live over in Solihull. Very boring!"

"Nonsense!" David lied. "We all think our own jobs are boring. It's the other man's grass syndrome. I painted an official commemorative portrait of the person they refer to as Red Leader in the Red Arrows last month – a chap called Gordon Kray. When I presented him with it at Scampton RAF base, he said, quite sincerely, that he'd give anything to be able to paint like me. He'd dabbled for years but was talentless at it, you see. I stood there, speechless. I had to remind him that he was leader of the blooming Red Arrows."

"Point taken," replied Gary, "but I bet he'd never dreamt of being a blasted accountant!"

David could not argue with this. Instead, he produced a tiny black and white photograph from his wallet and showed it to those present. It was a picture of Gary, David and Mally at the school play, dressed in what appeared to be Baco-foil. Mally was wearing a tin hat with a streak of lightning crudely painted on it, and David was brandishing a wooden ray gun with a flashing light at the end. Behind them, a Dalek looked on menacingly.

"The school play, summer nineteen-sixty-five," David announced. "They say what goes around comes around. "Doctor Who is back on the telly again, and Subbuteo is making a come-back. Have you seen the new series, vicar?"

Now it was the Reverend Spittle's turn to choke - his foodstuff of choice being the tuna vol-au-vent.

"No, I was, erm, never a fan of Doctor Who."

Gary flashed David a look that spoke volumes. Now David deemed it best to change the subject. Vicars didn't generally resort to punching members of their flock, but this one was also a trained pugilist.

"Anyway, who else has turned up? I can see old Margaret Parsons over there. Did she ever become a policewoman in the end?"

"Damned right she did," growled Mr Lewis. "She did me for speeding in nineteen-eighty-two. Cheeky minx, after I helped her pass her eleven plus as well!"

"And where's Mally Lobes. I can't see him anywhere? Late as usual I suppose."

"Ah!" replied the Reverend Spittle, slowly recovering from his choking fit. "Late is perhaps the right word. I have some bad news for you, I'm afraid. I presided over his funeral last year."

David looked at Gary. He raised his fingers to his lips, and then clasped his mouth in shock.

"Oh no. Oh Jeez! He was only fifty-one. What happened?"

"A heart attack, caused by smoking, I believe."

Life was indeed very unpredictable. The octogenarian teacher and the polio victim were still going strong. Dear old Mally was physically the most robust of the three friends, but had departed first, and was buried by the man who once used to bully him in the school playground. It was a funny old world. David, his eyes welling up, raised his glass of Shiraz and proposed a toast.

"To Mally. God bless him!"

"God bless him!" echoed the Reverend Spittle and a sad-looking Mr Lewis in unison.

"Bless him!" added Gary, swigging off his Chablis. As a confirmed atheist, there were certain words he tended to omit from such toasts.

The little group was in serious danger of becoming maudlin, so the arrival of a young, attractive, bespectacled blonde woman in her thirties was a welcome distraction.

"Just doing the rounds," she smiled. "I'm Mary Westbury, the head teacher."

The lady's mobile, buried deep within her handbag, began to play a turgid, mechanical version of Greensleeves.

"Excuse me will you," she whispered, and stepped back from the group to take her call. After five minutes or so of debate about budgets, meetings and key stages with an anonymous colleague, she walked off and began introducing herself to another party.

"Oh well!" smiled David sadly. "Hello, goodbye."

"She's a busy woman," observed the Reverend Spittle. "It's not like it was when we were here, I'm afraid. These head teachers have to be glorified business managers rather than spiritual leaders nowadays. I phoned her last week about some children who have been throwing litter around in the churchyard. They were from this school, because the litter consisted of old Brierley Bank exercise books and the like. Dave Grainger, my gardener, actually saw them, and they were wearing the Brierley Bank uniform. One kid actually threw a cobble at him and used language you wouldn't believe a small kid would even know!"

"So Dave Grainger was in grave danger!" interrupted David, flippantly.

"Very good, yes!" admitted the Reverend. "So I phoned our Miss Westbury, and she explained to me that the kids were not her responsibility once off the school premises. I told her that I realized this, but asked if she could do something anyway, as I felt it was her *moral* responsibility, if nothing else. She curtly explained to me that she was a head teacher, not a social worker. They were wearing her school's uniform, I pointed out, but she said that it was the responsibility of the parents, and nothing to do with her after four o'clock."

"Flipping heck!" frowned Gary. "Can you imagine Sam Perriman talking like that?"

"Or that Mr Lewis?" asked Mr Lewis.

"Exactly!" agreed the Reverend Spittle. "And on that note, folks, I have to disappear, I'm afraid. I have to visit a lonely old man who's just lost his beloved wife after sixty years. Lovely to see you all." And with that, he was gone.

"Well," said David, shaking his head in disbelief, "we've just witnessed a miracle, folks. The words 'spots', 'leopard' and 'change' spring to mind. Amazing!"

A tall, twenty-something gentleman in an Adidas tracksuit strode over and apologized for his intrusion.

"Good evening folks," he beamed, "I'm Mr Richards, the P.E. teacher, and just-about-everything-else teacher as well, come to that. Which one of you is Gary Leyton?"

"I am, unless you're the man from the VAT office," quipped Gary. These accountants were a laugh a minute when they got started.

"Ah, good!" smiled the teacher.

"Do you know what Adidas stands for?" asked David, pointing to the logo on the gentleman's tracksuit.

"No, I don't actually."

"It stands for Adolf Dassler. You can see why they shortened it. Anyway, carry on!"

"Ahem, okay. Gary, we have a little surprise for you. Gents, if you'll kindly walk this way please."

David, Mr Lewis and Gary and followed the teacher to the other end of the room, while the headmistress asked the remaining guests to do likewise. Mr Richards halted at a large foldaway table near to the stage and whisked away a thin dust sheet that was covering it. Underneath was a rectangle of tightly-stretched green baize marked out like a football pitch, with two plastic goals at either end. Two white cardboard boxes rested on the table – one labelled Brierley Bank Celtic and the other Aston Villa. Next to them was a framed black and white photograph showing an eleven-year-old Gary Leyton with an inordinately proud look on his face, struggling to hold a wonky cup aloft. Behind him stood a wiry-haired teacher in a plain blue and logo-free tracksuit and a stocky boy with huge, bat-like ears. To the left of them and partially out of the frame, a young, stick-thin lad with a Brylcreemed Adolf Hitler hairdo was clapping enthusiastically.

Gary picked up the photograph and stared at it. Then, something embarrassing, yet rather touching happened. He began to cry. David Day flung an arm around him, and before long, he was fighting back the tears too. Mr Richards, meanwhile, opened the two boxes and began to place the two teams of players on the pitch. Someone had even taken the trouble, albeit somewhat ham-fistedly, to paint the Brierley Bank team in green hoops.

"Ladies and gentlemen," announced the teacher. "May I introduce Gary Leyton, the inaugural winner of the Brierley Bank Junior School Subbuteo F.A. Cup. We thought it would be good to take you all down Memory Lane tonight, and relive that wonderful afternoon forty-two years ago, when I was, let's see… minus fourteen years old. By all accounts, it was a landmark year. It was the year the Beatles released 'Help!', the year the school discovered that their sports' cups were worth a small fortune, and the year Brierley Bank Celtic, a lowly Sunday league team, beat Aston Villa by thirty-seven goals to nine. Just for a bit of fun, we're going to ask our original winner to play his old friend, David here, in the absence of Robert Glazier, who now lives in Spain, for five minutes a side, just to see if he's still got the knack!"

The small, bemused audience gathered around. David strolled up to the table, picked up Gary's centre forward and kissed it theatrically.

"Why's he kissing your player?" asked young Mr Richards, intrigued.

"Oh, that's his granddad, that's why," Gary informed him, matter-of-factly.

Mr Lewis was handed a whistle and asked to revive his original role as referee. Within the space of a few flicks, it was obvious to all present that Gary still possessed the magic touch, just as David still lacked it. After a spirited but mercifully short encounter, Gary emerged victorious by seven goals to nil.

"I give up," grinned David, chucking the tiny plastic football at his opponent's head in frustration. "You were always the best at football in our school."

The onlookers applauded enthusiastically and were about to retreat to the drinks table once more, but Mr Richards appealed for order.

"Folks, just one last thing before I leave you in peace. Nineteen-sixty-five was also the year we first allowed our pupils to write their own school play, and who amongst our older guests can forget the dramatic masterpiece that was 'Miss Kettle and the Dalek Egg', written by a pupil from 6L named David Day, with a little help from his friends. David, if you would kindly look to your left, please."

The hall's double-doors burst open, and in glided a bright red hardboard Dalek, its lights flashing and its sink plunger gyrating furiously.

"EXTERMINATE!" it cackled maniacally, twisting this way and that. Thankfully, the Reverend Spittle had been spared the spectacle. Had his heart been weak, it may well have proved too much for him. It was true that he now worked tirelessly for God, but one presumed that he was in no particular hurry to actually meet his employer face to face.

David, doubled up with laughter, dissolved into near hysterics as it circled around him, screaming "You will be *DESTROYED!*"

He intercepted the battered old robot and flung his arms around it, hugging it with such intensity that the unknown and unsung teacher within must have feared for his life.

"Why's he hugging the Dalek," asked Mr Richards. It was a fair question, after all.

"Oh, I'm not hugging a Dalek – I'm hugging my dad!" explained David, removing his spectacles and wiping away a bittersweet tear.

THE END

I was recently contacted by Mrs Gwen Perry, widow of Samuel Perry, who was the inspiration for my fictional headmaster, Mr Perriman. Gwen is ninety-one years old and absolutely wonderful! We met in December 2009 and she kindly lent me a few old photographs, which caused a few bittersweet tears, I can tell you. The one above shows the 1963 football team. Mr Perry is on the right, Mr Weston (not featured in this particular tale) on the left, and Mr Lewis in the middle. Sadly, unlike the fictional Mr Lewis, he died aged fifty-four of a heart attack - my age when I began this story. You will note that I wasn't selected for the team, as usual, but Robert Glaze (front row, second from right) always was, and he later ended up at Aston Villa I believe. He was also instrumental in establishing the Quarry Bank Subbuteo League, which inspired me to write this book. And you thought I made it all up!

Incidentally, I wonder if that little silver trophy is still knocking about in someone's attic. No reason for asking – just curious.

Those of you who have read a David Day book will know how addictive they can become. At first, you think you can take them or leave them – you are an adult with a modicum of willpower, after all, and no mere book is going to rule your life. Quite soon though, you realize that you've started reading a quick chapter while you're in the bath or the lavatory. From there it is but a short step to the torch under the bed sheets at midnight and the paperback hidden inside your desk at the office. You'll find yourself reading the final chapter extra slowly to make it last longer, savouring every word and even reading good bits twice. Then, when you can stall no further and the book is finished, you will go through an awful mourning process, whereupon an intense craving will kick in. You'll need more and you'll need it NOW. Bad-tempered due to the crippling withdrawal symptoms, you'll probably complain that the author isn't nearly prolific enough for your voracious appetite, and begin to call him rude names. Extreme cases have even been known to try and climb the walls in anguish. Friends will turn against you because you will insist on regurgitating the plots *ad nauseam* while they're trying to watch television. It will get so bad that you might seriously consider a spell in a rehab clinic, or maybe a course of hypnotism.

Well, help is at hand. Why not join the David Day Fan Club? It's a bit like Alcoholics Anonymous. You sit around in a circle and confess, "My name is Deirdre Sponge and I'm a David Day fanatic." (Obviously, you don't say this if your name i*sn't* Deirdre Sponge. That was just an example.) Then the others get up and hug you, with a bit of luck.

If you email me at gt@geofftristram.co.uk I'll keep your name on file and let you know when a new book is due to be released into the wild. Unlike other authors who are now too important – people such as J.K. Rowling and William Shakespeare for example, I promise to be approachable, grateful, humble, and always write

179

back. That's with the proviso that you tell me my books are great, of course. I don't want any sour-faced old scrooges writing in to tell me I'm rubbish and that I deserve to be horse-whipped on the steps of my club. Maybe I could cope if you've spotted a glaring error, or a bit you didn't think made perfect sense, but obviously, I'd prefer it if you to told me how a paragraph had made you wet yourself on the train, or prevented you from leaping off a high building to certain death. You can suggest things that David can get up to in future stories, if you wish. I might even write *you* into a book. After all, most of my characters are based on real people, believe it or not! Oops! Shouldn't have admitted that – now no-one will believe that legal disclaimer in the small print at the beginning.

Anyway, I'll leave it with you. The offer's there. You can lead a horse to water but you can't make it drink, as my Granny Bertha often attempted to say. I hope you've enjoyed 'The Hunt for Granddad's Head'. Next up is my brand new David Day tale, entitled 'David's Michelangelo, which sees our hero, now aged 48, teaming up with his old friend Laz again, and I can guarantee you won't be disappointed. I am absolutely thrilled with it, and delighted by the news that Pizza Express has agreed not only to sponsor it, but also to sell it! I have probably been eating at their restaurants now for twenty years or more, so I wouldn't like you to think that I'd added a few gratuitous plugs in the new book in order to squeeze a few quid out of them (even though I know it will appear that way). In fact, I set the first and last chapters of the new book in their Stourbridge branch because it suited the plot, and the sponsorship resulted from that, so there!

My big problem now is that I've used up my batch of ten ISBN numbers, so I've either got to call it a day or buy another ten, and they're not cheap, I can tell you. I can't imagine that I have another ten books left in me, and it's such a waste of money. Decisions, decisions!

Love to you all, Geoff Tristram.

Books by Geoff Tristram

A NASTY BUMP ON THE HEAD (PG rated)

Eleven-year-old David Day finds the curmudgeonly toy shop owner, Miss Kettle, murdered in her shop. He duly informs Scotland Yard, only to bump into her in Tenbury- Wells the following week.

MONET TROUBLE

First year art student David Day is persuaded to forge a Monet painting by the mysterious Lord Hickman, but unknown to either of them, several other artists have the same idea.

VINCENT GOUGH'S VAN

An art college murder mystery of Shakespearian proportions, littered with psychic sewing teachers, psychopathic students and Sapphic assassins.

THE CURSE OF TUTTON COMMON

David sets about trying to improve Britain's worst museum, and ably assisted by a cat named Hitlerina, he discovers an ancient Egyptian tomb in South Staffordshire.

PAINTING BY NUMBERS

Thirty-year-old David is having a mid-life crisis, made worse by the fact that his art studio has exploded, and the ninety-year-old 'paint by numbers' enthusiast he has befriended is not what he seems.

STEALING THE ASHES

Forty–year-old David Day overhears two Australian cricketers plotting to steal the Ashes, and, ably hampered by Laz, he tries his best to thwart their plans.

Written and soon to be published;

DAVID'S MICHELANGELO

David's best friend Laz opens an Italian restaurant in Tutton on Stour, and asks David to paint the ceiling, which sets off an incredible chain of events that threatens to rock the art-world to its core.

...and two new novels featuring a new hero!

THE CURIOUS TALE OF THE MISSING HOOF

Writer Adam Eve hires a pantomime horse costume, but forfeits his deposit when he loses one of the hooves. His obsessive efforts to locate it create mayhem!

MR. MAORI GOES HOME

Adam Eve's hell-raising uncle has died and left him a substantial amount of money – on condition that he returns a rare Maori carving to New Zealand.

For more information, email gt@geofftristram.co.uk

181